I0833615

THE CROSS AND THE HAMMER:

A TALE OF THE DAYS OF THE VIKINGS

OTHER BOOKS IN THE
H. BEDFORD-JONES UNIFORM
EDITION LIBRARY:

Adventures of a Professional Corpse

Colonel Flea

Conquest: The Story of Pierre Radisson, Founder of the Hudson Bay Company

Gimlet Eye Gunn

Invitation to a Crime: Further Adventures of Denis Burke

The Life of Pinky Jenkins, Volume 1

The Mardi Gras Mystery

Red Runes of China

Thady Shea's Saga

Tyrone of New Orleans

H. BEDFORD-JONES

THE CROSS AND THE HAMMER

A TALE OF THE DAYS OF THE VIKINGS

H. BEDFORD-JONES

ALTUS PRESS • 2016

PUBLISHING HISTORY

The Cross and the Hammer: A Tale of the Days of the Vikings was originally published by The David C. Cook Publishing Company in 1912.

THANKS TO

Gerd Pircher

Printed in the United States of America.

TABLE OF CONTENTS

FOREWORD

This is a story about the very real people and events; if ever you chance to read the old Sagas of Norway you will come upon most of the characters of this tale. The viking age was not Christian, it was full of the clash of arms and of unknightly deeds, yet its story is vitally interesting.

The Hammer of Thor, the War-god of northern Europe, did not yield to the Cross of Christ without a struggle, and the story of Norway's conversion is intensely dramatic. King Hakon the Good, a foster-son of the English King Athelstan, was forced to recant his faith in order to hold his throne; King Olaf Triggveson lost his kingdom, or rather gave it up, at Svolde Sound, because he refused to do the like; and King Olaf the Thick, who followed him, fell beneath the heathen weapons of his subjects, becoming the patron saint of Norway.

It was the first King Olaf who broke the power of the old gods and who introduced Christianity into his realm. Short as was his reign, he was the greatest king Norway ever had. He built the first church in the land, and sent the first missionaries to Iceland; during his reign Thangbrand, the priest, won that island to the true faith.

Many of the incidents narrated are taken direct from the Sagas, and although King Olaf is said to have died at Svolde, the story of his escape is well authenticated; I give his own words in refusing to win back his kingdom. He went to Rome and the Holy Land and held rule there under the Crusader Kings of Jerusalem, dying fifty years later. King Edward the Confessor used to have the story of his life chanted to his court once every year, upon his death being reported in England during that king's reign.

—H. Bedford-Jones

NOTES

"bonders."—This word is used in the Sagas to represent the free farmers of Norway, who held their lands from the king, or owned them; they were subject only to the orders of the king or his Jarls, and are equivalent to our own "farmers," except that they had special rights and privileges.

"scat"—A fine or any other penalty which might be imposed on an offender by an assembly of the people. The scat was usually a fine of money, lands, or goods.

"skoal"—This plain word corresponds to our own "Hurrah!" It means both long life, good health, and joy, and is still used in Norway in that sense.

I have avoided the use of many words which are usually retained in the translations of the old Sagas. Nearly all the facts about which the story of Sigurd Fairhair is woven are historical, and are taken from the Heimskringla, and the Saga of King Olaf by the Abbot Berg Sokkason. Both histories were compiled from the accounts of eye-witnesses of the events contained therein, to a great extent, and especially was this true with the life of Olaf Triggveson.

—*The Author.*

CHAPTER I

HOW THE VOW WAS MADE

THE GREAT hall of the Danish kings at Leira was filled to overflowing on this autumn evening of the year 994, for King Harald Gormson had fallen in battle some weeks before, and his son Svein Twyskiegge, of Forkbeard, was celebrating his accession feast in the hall of his fathers.

Around the town lay a whole city of tents and brush huts, for besides the Danish lords present, sixty ships had come from Jomsborg, bearing the noblest of the famous Viking brotherhood, under their chiefs Jarl Sigvald and Bui the Thick. Visitors and Danes were clad in their bravest array, and both town and camp presented a scene of the gayest festivity.

Within, the hall was hung with ancient arms and trophies of the chase, the floor was strewn with a thick layer of fresh rushes, and the long tables were heaped high with dishes. At one end of the hall sat King Svein, with his chiefs and the Jomsborg nobles, while above them towered the high-seat or throne of the king; along the hall were ranged the vikings and men of Denmark, with Queen Gunhild and her ladies sitting at the far end.

Servants flitted in and out, bearing food and horns of ale, while in the center of the hall, between the tables and before the seat of the king, sat two skalds, singing to the music of their harps the great deeds of King Harald and of his son, the new king.

Presently, as the hunger of the throng was somewhat appeased, all began to wonder what vow the king would make, for it was the custom that at the heirship feast the new king should make a vow to do some great and noble deed.

Seated near Queen Gunhild as guests of honor were two boys, one fair and ruddy-cheeked, the other darker and with very quick, bold eyes. The latter, Vagn Akison, was a nephew of Bui, the Jomsborg chief, and grandson of Palnatoki, the founder of the viking brotherhood; although he was only seventeen, he and his cousin Sigurd were already well known for the prowess.

Sigurd Fairhair, who was a year younger than Vagn, was in high spirits to-night, for a little before King Svein had given him a very fine sword, and he was proud of it.

Glancing over at him with a smile, Queen Gunhild said, "Sigurd, have you shown Astrid your new sword?"

"Of course he has," replied Astrid, her niece, who sat beside Sigurd, and her dark eyes gleamed with fun. "He is going to try its edge on the big pine tree near the harbor to-morrow!"

At this sally a laugh went up, and Vagn cried, "Be careful not to bring down the tree into the harbor, Sigurd! It would be a pity to sink all our best ships!"

Sigurd reddened, and retorted, "Well, I never aroused the whole camp just because a pig was wandering around in the bushes!"

This turned the laugh on his cousin, who had wakened the camp the night before, mistaking a pig for a spy, and even the Queen joined heartily in the merriment.

Suddenly a silence fell on the tables, for King Svein had arisen and was holding in both hands a great silver bowl. Amid a dead hush he drained it, handed it to an attendant, and stepped to the high-seat. Grasping an arm of this, the king turned.

"Here, as I ascend the throne of my father Harald, I vow that with the help of God I will lead my fleet to the land of England, and ere three winters have passed I will chase King Ethelred from the land and sit in his throne!"

As King Svein took his seat a low murmur of astonishment ran around the hall, followed by a tremendous shout of "Skoal! Skoal!" for this was a great vow to be fulfilled.

"See how pale the Queen is," whispered Astrid to Sigurd. "The vow must have surprised her also."

Indeed, Queen Gunhild had turned white, for the King's vow meant that a great war would be undertaken, and how it would end no man could tell. Before Sigurd could reply, Jarl Sigvald arose and called for silence.

"Men of Denmark and Jomsborg," he said slowly, in his deep voice, the light glinting on his dark, strong face and black eyes, "I also would make a vow, and no light one. As you all know, Jarl Hakon, a heathen man and doubly a traitor, rules Norway while the rightful king, Tryggvee's son, is a wanderer or mayhap dead. This then is my vow: that I go to Norway ere three winters pass, take the rule from the hands of Jarl Hakon, and drive him from the land."

Sigvald sat down, amid a dead hush of amazement; but it was broken by a shout from young Vagn Akison.

"Skoal, Jarl Sigvald, skoal!"

Then what a cheer went up! Ere it subsided, Sigvald's brother, Thorkel the Tall; leaped to his feet and swore to follow the Jarl; Bui the Thick joined him, and amid fresh cheers, Vagn, from the other end of the hall, cried:

"I, too! And ere I return I will slay Thorkel Leira, the villain who betrayed my father to his death!"

"Skoal!" shouted Sigurd, excitedly, "I'm with you, Vagn!"

As the tumult subsided, the Queen looked at Vagn and Sigurd sadly. "You are rash boys, you two! Do you realize what blood and tears these oaths will cost?"

Sigurd answered her respectfully. "Noble Gunhild, that may well be; yet Jarl Hakon is an evil man and a pagan, as is Thorkel. At any rate, I won't have to try my new sword on the tree, now!" His keen gray eyes twinkled.

The Queen made no reply, however, and sat watching King Svein; but Astrid whispered:

"I think that was splendid! I wish I could go, too!"

Vagn laughed. "You'd be a fine one! Why, the first war-horn would send you down below trembling!"

"It wouldn't either!" retorted the girl indignantly. "I can shoot better than you or Sigurd, either of you!"

"Good! I challenge you to a match to-morrow," cried Sigurd. "We'll go over to the shore beyond the harbor, where no one will interrupt, and if you best either of us I'll give you my trained falcon from France!"

"Then look out," laughed Astrid, "because I'm going to win the bird to-morrow morning!"

With this she arose and followed the Queen, who was leaving. The two boys, not wishing to join in the carouse that most of the vikings would keep up for the better part of the night, also left the hall and proceeded to their own tent.

"What think you of these vows, Sigurd?" asked Vagn, as they went along.

"Well, now that we have cooled down, it looks rather different," replied Sigurd, thoughtfully. "It is one thing for King Svein to conquer England, with the resources of a realm at his command, and another for Sigvald to conquer Norway with only the brother of Jomsborg behind him."

"But remember, Fairhair, we are Christians, while Hakon is a pagan and a traitor; that will make some difference, surely! My own vow was no hasty thing; I must avenge my father's death or else be disgraced forever."

Sigurd nodded thoughtfully, for he well knew that the fierce vikings would yield small obedience to a man who appeared unable to avenge the betrayal of his father. As they turned in at their tent, a man ran up, and Vagn recognized one of Bui's men in the moonlight.

"Hello, Egil, what is it?"

"I will lead my fleet to the land of England."

"You and Sigurd are wanted at council in Jarl Sigvald's big tent," panted the man.

Without delay, the boys followed him to the large tent of the Jarl. Here they found all the Jomsborg leaders assembled, and took their places beside Bui of Bornholm, who was speaking as they entered.

"It was a rash vow, Sigvald, but we cannot back out, and it may well be that we shall win great honor in the effort, win or lose. Our vikings are the best warriors in the world to-day, and we will at least give a hard battle to Hakon and his son Eirik."

A murmur of assent ran around the tent, and Sigvald arose.

"Brothers, I was over-hasty in the vow, but it cannot be helped. This is my counsel; that since the attempt must be made, we make it without delay, send for the rest of our men, and strike at Norway's capital without delay. What think you?"

Vagn stepped forward. "I will answer for my father's ships and men. Let us strike before Hakon can meet us; we have the pick of our men here, with most of our ships. We can leave here at the end of the week, wait at Limafiord for the rest of our men, then sweep up to Thrandheim."

"Good for you, Vagn!" cried his uncle. "Men say that I am somewhat stout, but my friends never complain of my weight in battle!" Everyone laughed, for although Bui deserved his nickname, he was one of the greatest warriors of the day. "I'll let Sigurd here go with you, if you want him," he continued, and the boy's heart leaped with joy, for this was indeed just what he did want.

Jarl Sigvald smiled. "Then is it agreed that we go from here to Limafiord on the fourth day?"

"Yes!" The answer was accompanied by a clash of weapons, as the chiefs struck sword and spear on shield, and the council was over, although most of the leaders remained to talk over details and despatch a messenger to Jomsborg at once.

The boys returned to their tent, however, and as they dropped off to sleep the shouts of "Skoal! Skoal!" drifted faintly to them from the town, and they knew that the vikings and the Danes were still making vows, some of which they would bitterly repent in the morning.

CHAPTER II

THE SHOOTING-MATCH

EARLY NEXT morning the boys were afoot, and after a hasty breakfast beside a camp fire they took their bows and quivers and started for town.

Astrid lived with Queen Gunhild at the Kings' Hall, and thither they directed their steps. Early as it was, the place was thronged with servants, who were laying fresh rushes in the hall and putting the place in order for the day. Seeing a house-carl pass, with his clipped hair and golden collar, Sigurd called him and sent him to ask if the Lady Astrid was ready.

Five minutes later Astrid herself appeared, bearing bow and quiver, and joined them with a cheery, "Good-morning, my vikings! Has your rash resolution cooled off yet?"

"Small chance of, that," replied Vagn, his half-grave, half-humorous eyes lighting up in a quick smile.

"My falcon is ready to change owners," added Sigurd, "but then there is no chance for that to-day, of course."

"Oh, indeed!" Astrid's dark eyes flashed gayly. "That remains to be seen, my lord of Jomsborg and Bornholm!"

Talking and laughing, they started off, leaving the town behind and cutting across the fields to the harbor. There, as they came to the brow of the hill, they paused. Far below lay the great fleet, the sixty Jomsborg ships and those of the assembled Danish lords, their shield-rims glittering in the morning sun, their dragon-prows and high carved sterns gilded or painted in bright array.

Astrid caught her breath in admiration. "Oh, how wonderful it is to be a viking! I wish I were a boy!"

The other two laughed. "It is not so very wonderful," smiled Sigurd. "I think it is hard work. Every morning the drilling and practice in arms, the weapons to be rubbed up—and the rowing! Whew, my back hurts even to think of those low, heavy oars!"

"There's our ship, with the gilded prow," pointed Vagn, to a large long-ship apart from the rest. "Sigurd talks a lot about work, but he is equal to any man in the fleet with sword and shield, save his father, or the Jarl—"

"Or yourself," broke in his cousin quickly. "However, let's get on; I'm anxious to decide the fate of my falcon."

They left the road, and after walking two or three miles, came out on a lonely stretch of shore, wild and rocky. Vagn had brought an old wooden shield with him, and he set this up as target on a large rock a hundred feet distant.

"Do you shoot first," ordered Astrid. "I'll go next, then Vagn."

Sigurd nodded, and selected an arrow. Stringing his bow, he laid the shaft and pulled the string to his ear. Twang! The arrow was buried deep in the shield, just above the center boss of iron.

"Good enough!" cried Vagn, running forward, but Astrid only smiled and raised her bow. The string twanged, and an answering echo came back as the arrow glanced off and the shield fell backward.

"Hurrah!" cried Vagn, picking it up. "Full on the iron boss! But you can't do it again!"

Sigurd ran forward to see also, and as they examined the shield, a sudden cry startled them. Turning, they saw Astrid struggling with three men, while more appeared coming from behind a corner of the cliff.

"Norsemen and spies!" exclaimed Sigurd, and without an instant's hesitation he picked up Astrid's arrow and ran forward, fitting it to his bow.

"Your sword!" called Vagn, tearing the peace-bands from his own weapon as he ran. A shout answered him, and the Norseman ran forward to meet Sigurd. A spear whizzed by his head, and he loosed the bow.

The foremost viking fell with a clash, and as the others paused Sigurd tore the peace-bands from his sword. Next instant he was surrounded, struggling, striking, and he realized that more and more men had appeared from behind the cliff.

Now a blade gleamed beside him, and Vagn's voice sounded in his ear. One man was down—two; but others filled their places, and a heavy axe was poised over Sigurd. As it fell the boy darted in beneath the blow, and his sword fell on the viking's shoulder; but at that instant something crashed on his light steel cap, and he knew no more.

Sigurd awoke with a dull pain in his head, to find his arms tightly bound and the midday sun beating down on him. Raising his head, Fairhair saw that he lay on the forecastle of a small ship, with Vagn beside him, wounded in the shoulder and unconscious.

He saw nothing of Astrid, and a burning thirst consumed him; with a great effort he rose to a sitting position and looked around. They were out at sea, and the land lay far behind them; in the stern and waist of the ship were fifteen or twenty Norsemen.

"That was a stiff crack I gave you, lad, but the steel cap saved your skull," sounded a voice, and Sigurd twisted around. Behind him stood a dark man with an unpleasant face and straw-colored hair; evidently he was the leader, for he had just come out of the cabin.

Sigurd tried to speak, but his tongue was dry, and the man laughed. "Here, Thord," he called, "bring a horn of water."

One of the men in the waist took a horn and filled it from the cask beside the mast, handing it up to the leader, who put it to the boy's lips. Sigurd drank greedily, and then the other threw a few drops over Vagn, who opened his eyes.

He struggled to rise, with a sharp cry.

"Thorkel Leira! I—" The effort was too much for him, and he fell back again. Their captor smiled sneeringly.

"He is in a bad way to fulfill his vow, eh?" This was the man whom Vagn had sworn to kill, the betrayer of his father! As he realized this, Sigurd's head cleared.

"Why have you attacked us? Who are you?" he asked indignantly.

Thorkel laughed again. "Vagn, there, seemed to know my face! You two and the girl, whom I take to be Gunhild's niece, will make a nice gift to Jarl Hakon! Great boasts, great boasts!"

Sigurd flushed. As he looked at the viking, his heart gave a sudden leap, for, framed in the cabin doorway behind, he saw the face of Astrid, her finger on her lips. Making no sign, he answered the leader calmly.

"In that case, leave us alone till we get to Thrandheim." As he said this, Sigurd lay down again, turning his back on Thorkel. The latter sneered, and stepped to the edge of the forecastle, above the ship's waist. Sigurd opened his eyes, and saw Astrid making signs, and holding in her hand his sword.

Sigurd comprehended the plan instantly. He silently drew his feet up and gathered his muscles; Thorkel was giving orders, a few paces away, and paid no heed to him. The boy slowly rose to one knee; he saw Astrid run toward him, and at the same instant he threw himself headfirst at Thorkel, striking him fairly in the waist.

The viking fell forward with a cry, and lay motionless on the deck beneath. Sigurd would have followed him over the low rail, but for a hand that gripped his bound arms and stayed him; then he felt the bonds cut and a sword pushed into his hand.

"Hold the ladder," panted the girl, "while I arouse Vagn."

Sigurd sprang to the top of the narrow ladder that led up from the deck below just as the surprised men seized their weapons. An arrow tore through his hair; another followed, but Sigurd parried it with his blade, and another after it. This was an old viking exercise, and the boy felt no fear; but with a cry of dismay Astrid ran to the cabin, quickly returning with a shield.

"Here, this will help you!" Sigurd grasped it just in time to ward off a spear, and now the first man was on the ladder. He held a shield above his head, but Sigurd swung his sword and brought it down with all his might. The keen weapon sheared through the tough bull's hide, and the man fell back among his comrades.

Thord, who had brought the water, now made a dash, coming up the ladder three steps at a time, and wielding an axe. As he reached the top Sigurd drove his sword, but too late; the axe descended on his shield and bore him to his knees. Again the weapon whirled above him, and Thord staggered backward with a hoarse cry, clearing the ladder in his fall.

Springing up, Sigurd saw Astrid behind him, bow in hand, and Vagn, pale but determined, stepped to his side. Those below drew back, and the boys saw them reviving Thorkel, who was stunned by his fall. Sigurd leaned on his sword.

"Look here, Vagn, we can't keep this up all day; one or two good showers of arrows will finish us."

Vagn pointed to the cabin. "We can hold that against them all, and Astrid says that food and water are inside."

Sigurd laughed. "You look like a Valkyrie, Astrid! I owe you thanks for my life, too—but what is Thorkel up to?"

"Back—back to the cabin!" cried Astrid. "They are climbing around the bow to take us from behind!"

A glance showed them half a dozen men climbing through the bow under the dragon's head up to the forecastle. It was useless to try to hold the whole fore-deck, so the two boys and Astrid ran to the cabin, shut the heavy door, and bolted it securely. There was no window, and only one or two high loopholes gave fresh air to those within.

"What chance have we of rescue?" asked Astrid, sitting down on a pile of furs.

"Little enough," replied Vagn, moodily, while Sigurd threw himself down beside her. "No one knows where we went, and we won't be missed till noon. It must be about three hours past that now."

The Norsemen, realizing the futility of trying to break in, made no sign; and the afternoon slowly wore away. The ship was bearing north under full sail, and all three captives realized that it was only a matter of time before they would have to give up.

Evidently the Norsemen had been spying on the Danes. Vagn had been struck down by a glancing blow, and all three had been taken to the ship, which left the land at once. Astrid had been left unbound, and had taken advantage of the opportunity as soon as Sigurd became conscious.

Toward evening a rap sounded on the door, and the voice of Thorkel called to them:

"Vagn Akison! Can you hear me?"

CHAPTER III

JARL HAKON OF NORWAY

"WELL ENOUGH," replied Vagn, "what is it?"

"I suppose you see that you cannot hold out for ever; but it would be needless trouble for my men to batter in the door. To-morrow we will meet Jarl Hakon, and if you give yourselves up in peace I will not bind you."

"What shall we do?" whispered Vagn. "It is true that we cannot hold out here."

"Do!" exclaimed Astrid. "Would you trust your father's betrayer? Wait till we meet Hakon, that will be time enough to give up!"

Vagn raised his voice. "We wish naught to do with traitors, Thorkel. Let Jarl Hakon speak with us; till then we will bide."

Thorkel made no answer, and they heard him move away. The three captives ate some of the food, drank a little stale water, and with nightfall the boys took watch and watch, leaving the single couch to Astrid.

Toward morning, however, the latter awoke and insisted on doing her share of the watching; so Sigurd, dead tired, yielded up his watch and dropped off to sleep. The boys were now suffering from their wounds, but they had refused to let Astrid bind them up, as this was strictly against the laws of the Jomsvikings.

These fierce men were trained with the greatest strictness, indeed, and death was the penalty for the slightest infraction of their laws. Wounds might not be bound up, and no pain might be complained of; for suffering was only part of the long training that made the Jomsborg brotherhood the most terrible fighters in the world.

Both boys were wakened by a jar that shook the ship, and they found the sun well up. "What was that shock?" they cried, in alarm.

"Another ship," replied Astrid. "I can see nothing, but I heard the sound of oars and voices."

Springing to the loopholes, they found that they could see nothing; but the sound of excited talking came to them, and in a few moments steps advanced quickly to the door.

"Ho, Vagn Akison! Astrid of Vendland! Open!"

Astrid seized Vagn's arm. "It is Jarl Hakon! I know his voice well!"

Without hesitation, Sigurd, sheathing his sword, threw open the door. There in the sunlight stood a man of lofty stature, magnificently armed and with beard and hair as sunny as that of Sigurd; but his face was gloomy, and his eyes quick and shifty.

"Do you yield to me?" he asked quietly.

Astrid laughed. "So you war against girls, Jarl? Well, I suppose I must surrender!"

The Jarl smiled, and laid his hand on her hair. "Keep the bow, child; you have done nobly and well. Come to my own ship."

As they followed him down the ladder and over the side, Sigurd saw that Hakon's hair was streaked with gray, and that he walked stiffly as from old wounds. Beside Thorkel's ship lay another, a splendid warship, and as they climbed over the bulwarks the two ships were cast apart. Hakon led the way to his cabin, and said, kindly:

"Sit you down and fear not. Thorkel has told me the tale of the vows, especially that of yours, Vagn Akison. By the hammer of Thor, your comrades will have tough work if they think to take Norway from me!" He smiled grimly.

"Jarl," exclaimed Astrid, "was it by your orders that we have been attacked? Remember that Svein is my uncle!"

Hakon nodded. "I am sorry, indeed, that you were taken; you will be returned unharmed later, with whatever scat Svein thinks just. But who are you, Fairhair?"

Sigurd laughed. "That is truly what men call me, Jarl; my name is Sigurd Buisson."

Hakon whistled in surprise. "So! Then I have two good hostages! All the better; I will take you up to Thrandheim with me, but have no fear, for you will be well treated—at least for the present."

With this Hakon left the cabin, giving it up to them, and the voyage began. The boys were indeed treated well, their weapons were left them, and had it not been for the surrounding circumstances they would have enjoyed themselves immensely.

That night they made the southern end of Norway, for the ship was pushed on with all speed, both of sail and oars. Jarl Hakon was racing for his kingdom now, and no effort was spared to reach Thrandheim, Norway's capital, as soon as might be.

Next morning they landed at Howes, and Hakon sent speedy messengers north over the mountains to his son Jarl Eirik, who was in Raumarike; and splitting up war arrows, dispatched them to all the chiefs near by as a token to gather men at once. Then, with fresh rowers, the ship hastened on as never ship had hastened before, for the realm of Norway was at stake.

The following evening they stopped at Raumsdale to send out the war-arrow and get new rowers; but they pushed on quickly, and on the third day sped up the Thrandheim Firth and reached the city just after sunset.

An immense crowd greeted them, for the news had sped fast, and they landed amid a great shouting and clash of arms. Jarl Hakon kept the boys with him, and sent Astrid to the King's Hall, where she would be given waiting-women and cared for as became her rank. Then, without going thither himself, he turned aside, followed by all the multitude, and proceeded to the great temple of Thor, the War-god.

Jarl Hakon was a pagan, believing firmly in the old gods of Norway, as indeed most of his subjects did. The Thrandheim temple was the greatest in the land, and Jarl Hakon, as ruler of the country, was the high-priest.

As they passed beneath the great stone doorway Sigurd Fairhair shivered, and Vagn whispered to him, "Firm, Sigurd, hold firm!"

Sigurd pressed his hand in reply. As they saw whither they were going, the boys had resolved not to take part in the worship of the heathen gods, for both were Christians. The temple was high and gloomy, and the torches lit it very poorly; but around the sides they could see statues of Odin the one-eyed, Freya the beautiful, and the other gods. At the end, opposite the doorway, stood a high altar before the golden statue of Thor, and Hakon slowly ascended the steps.

As he did so, the vikings, bonders, and townfolk fell on their knees, and beyond the altar Sigurd noticed the priests bringing in a white bull for sacrifice. Looking around, he saw that he and Vagn were the only ones standing; others saw it, too, and an angry mutter ran through the vast building, like the low gathering of a storm.

The two boys paled, but stood firm and erect, as Jarl Hakon uttered a short prayer to the war god. When his voice ceased, the mutter behind him swelled into a roar, with fierce shouts of "Kneel!" "Kneel!" "Death to the Christians!"

Hakon turned and raised his hand, the roar dying away at once. When he saw the cause of the tumult his face darkened.

"To your knees, to your knees! Would you insult Thor in his own temple?"

"We kneel to none save the white Christ," spoke out Sigurd boldly, though his heart beat fast.

Hakon's hand flew to his sword, and the crowd surged forward; then the Jarl's hand dropped, and he motioned to one of his men.

"Harald, take these two to the King's Hall and see that no harm comes to them, on your life. Go!"

Without a word the boys followed the man as he led the way out, their heads high and their hands on their swords. The Norsemen made way for them with muttered threats, but gaining the open air, their guide led them through the dark streets, and in a few minutes stopped at the Hall.

They were led to a room, and the door was bolted. At the rasp of the bolt Vagn broke silence.

"Whew! That was a close shave for us, old man! I was scared stiff when you answered Hakon!"

"So was I," admitted Sigurd, smiling. "But we are too valuable as hostages, so it didn't take much bravery. See here, are we going to stay with Hakon?"

"Not if we can help it," laughed Vagn. "I suppose we'll be watched closely, though, and then we must look out for Astrid."

Sigurd nodded. "Well, we'll see her in the morning. She is not in danger for the present, anyway."

Sigurd was mistaken, however, for they did not see Astrid for a week. They were closely confined to their room, and only on the sixth day following were they allowed to leave it. Their warder was the same who had led them from the temple the first night. As he came in on the sixth morning, he left the door open, and said:

"You are free of the town, but do not leave it. Jarl Hakon has gone, so you had best be watchful, as I am responsible for you."

"Where has Hakon gone? Is the Lady Astrid here?" asked Vagn.

"I know nothing of any Lady Astrid, but Jarl Hakon has gone south to More to raise men, and will return to meet Jarl Eirik, mayhap."

The two boys did not wait to learn more, but hastened out to the great hall, and there they found a woman who directed them to Astrid's room. Making their way thither, Astrid came to the door with a cry of joy.

"Oh, I thought you were dead! I saw Jarl Hakon once, but he was terribly busy and would tell me nothing. Where have you been?"

Vagn outlined their adventure at the temple, and told of their subsequent imprisonment in a few words.

"I never would have dared do that!" exclaimed Astrid as he finished. "To brave all those men that way! But come over here to this window and speak low; there are women in the next room."

Making sure that the door was fast, Sigurd and Vagn joined her at the window.

"Last night I heard two men talking out in the hall, and I listened. Jarl Eirik has gathered a great force of men from Raumadale and Halogaland and Thrandheim, and is fitting out an immense fleet in the greatest haste. Hakon is raising men in North and South More. Two nights ago, just before Hakon left, a messenger came from Eirik.

"Here is their plan. When Hakon has raised all the men he can, he will come north to meet Eirik, who is making his way south. They expect to have at least 150 longships when they combine forces, and intend to wait for your fleet in Hiorunga Bay and take them in a trap."

"A trap!" cried Sigurd. "With that great force?"

"Yes, because they are afraid of the men of Jomsborg, even with the numbers three to one. The peasants are to tell Jarl Sigvald that Hakon is in Hiorunga Bay with only one or two ships, and Sigvald and Bui will hurry in to capture him, thus falling among the whole fleet. Do you see?"

Sigurd's eyes flashed. "So Hakon is a traitor still! This is terrible, Vagn; in a trap like that no one will escape!"

"I am afraid not, Fairhair," Vagn shook his head sadly. "Sigvald will fall into it, for he is impetuous and hasty, as is your father also. I see only one thing to do."

"What is that?" cried the others, as he paused.

"That is for you, Sigurd, and me to steal a boat here in the harbor and sail out south. We have a bare chance of reaching Sigvald in time. Has Eirik reached Thrandheim yet?" He turned to Astrid.

"Not yet, but he is expected at any time."

"Then we may make it!" broke in Sigurd, excitedly.

Here Astrid drew herself up, and said, in a determined voice, "Wait a minute! If you go I go, too; you needn't think you can leave me behind!"

CHAPTER IV

THE RESCUE IN THE BAY

"THAT YOU sha'n't," replied Vagn. "We may be blown out to sea or captured by Eirik or Hakon; there is no telling. You are safe here."

Astrid's eyes flashed, and she cried, angrily, "I say I *will* go! If we are taken, I will be just as safe; and you two can handle a small boat in any sea."

"But, Astrid," objected Sigurd, in dismay, "at best it will take us three days, and—"

"So much the more need of another person. Now say no more." She set her mouth determinedly, and Vagn's opposition vanished in a peal of laughter.

"Come on," he cried gayly; "I would rather fight a dozen Norsemen than try to oppose you! We'll go down to the harbor now and see about a boat."

"You seem to think it is no more than a matter of picking out a boat and raising the sail," laughed Sigurd, as they left the hall.

"No," returned Vagn, "but there's no use thinking about obstacles before they appear."

The streets were thronged with men from the countryside roundabout, and the armorers seemed to be doing a thriving business. No one paid any attention to the three, and they soon made their way to the waterside.

As they walked slowly along, looking at the ships in the harbor, Sigurd suddenly stopped.

"Hurrah! I believe that I have a better plan still!" he cried. "Do you see that ship over there with the yellow eyes painted in her prow?"

"What of her?" asked Vagn.

"Don't you remember? She was in Jomsborg a month since, and her captain is an old friend of Jarl Sigvald's. Why can't we get him to take us down below Hiorunga Bay to meet the fleet?"

"The very thing!" Astrid clapped her hands in delight. "I confess that it seemed well-nigh hopeless to make our way in a small boat without being captured or blown far out to sea. But suppose he won't take us?"

"He will," returned Vagn, "I remember his name—Ulf Ringsson, and he will be glad to help Sigvald. How shall we see him?"

"Do you take Astrid back to the hall, and I will row out in a small boat," replied Sigurd. "If any are watching us, we will throw them off that way."

So Astrid and Vagn turned back, and Sigurd sauntered about for a time, as if watching the shipping. Presently he wandered down to a boatman.

"Lend me your boat for an hour or two, my friend," he said, handing the man a coin.

"Willingly," responded the man, pushing out his craft and putting the oars into it. "Business is not so good these days; I fear that I may have to go with Jarl Eirik if I want to make money!"

"Better not," laughed Sigurd, "you might meet Jomsborg steel, and that would be bad luck."

The man chuckled as he shoved Sigurd off. "No danger, my lord! If I'm not here when you return, just pull the boat up and leave her."

Sigurd nodded, and pulled slowly from the shore. He did not head straight out to the ship, but visited other craft first, asking questions of their crews and appearing simply curious. After a little he reached the side of Ulf's ship, and slipping under the side opposite the shore, clambered over the rail.

As he set foot on the deck, a tall man rose and faced him. "Who are you and what do you want?"

Sigurd smiled and took off his fur cap. "I want Ulf Ringsson, and I am Sigurd Buisson of Bornholm."

Ulf grasped his hand with a cry of surprise, and led him to the cabin.

"The crew is ashore, but it is best to take no chances. Now what are you doing here? I heard you had been taken by Hakon."

The boy swiftly outlined his adventures, told of the trap that was to be laid for the Jomsborg fleet, and asked Ulf to help them.

"Of course, Sigurd, of course! I can stow you two and the Lady Astrid away comfortably, but if we are overhauled—well, my men are no fighters, you know!"

"We'll take our chance of that," replied Sigurd, thanking him warmly for his aid. "Now, when can you sail? Every minute counts."

"I know, but I can't possibly start sooner than the morning of the third day from now. Say midnight of the second night after this. My cargo is not all in, and it would look too suspicious altogether. But the 'Otter' is a fast ship, and we will get down the coast much faster than will Eirik with his warships."

"You can expect us then," said Sigurd. "Will you meet us on shore?"

"It will be better so," replied Ulf. "I will get the 'Otter' farther out before nightfall, and will wait for you opposite here with a small boat."

With a parting handshake Sigurd slipped over the side again, and rowed slowly through the shipping on his way back. As he passed a large ship, he saw that the sailors were making a clumsy effort to raise the sail. Indeed, from their looks he took them for newly raised levies from the country on their way to join Hakon, as the ship was a war vessel. He rested a moment, watching them with a smile; then it died away as he saw an officer, whose back was turned toward him, standing directly beneath the heavy spar that the men were hoisting.

"He'd better look out," thought Sigurd, "if those fellows lost their grip on the rope—ah, I thought so!"

For, even as the thought flashed through his mind, the rope had slipped loose from the men, and the yard fell, striking the officer a glancing blow and knocking him overboard.

With a shout Sigurd drove his oars into the water and reached the place where the man had gone down before the confused men on the ship could put out a boat. He could see nothing of the man, so, quickly throwing off his fur cap and cloak and unbuckling his sword-belt, Sigurd took a long breath and dived from the boat's side.

For an instant the ice-cold water paralyzed him; then, opening his eyes, the boy struck down. There, just beneath him, was the senseless face of—Thorkel Leira!

Sigurd checked his stroke. Why not leave this traitor and villain to his fate, so richly deserved? Why risk his own life for that of a worthless fellow such as Thorkel? But he only hesitated an instant; hastily gripping the man's hair, he made for the surface.

As they all knew Jarl Sigvald's ship by sight, Ulf steered toward that direction.

Although Sigurd was a good swimmer, he reached the air with a great sigh of relief, for he had been under water nearly a minute, and the water was too cold for comfort. Thorkel had been struck senseless and made no resistance.

As he emerged, a shout sounded in his ear, and there beside him was a small boat. His own skiff was not far, and after the men at his side hauled up Thorkel, he struck out for his own boat. Sigurd realized only too well that he did not want to be questioned, for any mishap now would ruin their plans of escape; so, paying no heed to the shouts of the Norsemen, he clambered over the stern of his craft, donned his fur coat hastily, and made for the shore.

He pulled up the boat and made off at once. His dripping clothes had already frozen, and the cloak hid most of them, so that he regained the hall without question. As he entered his room, Vagn greeted him with a cry of amazement when he threw off the cloak.

"What on earth—" he began, but Sigurd interrupted with a laugh.

"Water, rather, Vagn. Help me get these wet things off first."

Jarl Hakon had sent them a goodly supply of garments, and when Sigurd had changed to dry clothes he recounted the adventure to his cousin.

"Good for you, old man!" cried Vagn, as he finished. "I don't think that I would have resisted the temptation to let him drown and get rid of the wretch. Did any recognize you?"

Sigurd shook his head. "I got away too quickly, and Thorkel was senseless. The yard struck him on the shoulder, so I suppose he wasn't very badly hurt. Don't say anything to Astrid about it."

"Why not?" asked Vagn, in surprise.

"Well," Sigurd hesitated, "she would make a fuss about it, and—well, I really wish you wouldn't, old fellow!"

Seeing that Sigurd really wished it so, Vagn agreed, and they went to Astrid's room to tell her of their plans with Ulf.

Astrid greeted them with a laugh. "You changed pretty quickly, Sigurd," she said.

"Why, what do you mean?" Both boys stared at her.

"Oh, one of my maids just ran in and told me how some yellow-haired stranger rescued our old friend Thorkel down in the harbor, and ran off before they could find out who he was. So I knew that it must be Fairhair, here!"

"So it was, Astrid!" cried out Vagn. "If I'd been there I would have let the scoundrel drown!"

"No you wouldn't, Vagn," protested Sigurd. "You might kill him in fair fight, but you wouldn't let him drown without trying to save him!"

"Never mind," declared Astrid, looking at Sigurd, "it was a noble thing to do, Fairhair, and I am proud of you for it."

Sigurd blushed rosily, and hastily turned the conversation by describing his meeting with Ulf.

"By the way," added Vagn, "I found out something. At night our doors are locked and a man sleeps outside in the hall, before them. Hakon must think we are worth keeping!"

Sigurd thought it over. "The only way I can see is to entice our guard inside and tie him up, then go to Astrid's room and seize her guard before he can cry out. Any way, Astrid, be ready on the second night from this, about midnight, and we will get you somehow."

"We had best not be seen together in the meantime," cautioned the girl, "or someone may become suspicious."

Vagn nodded. "That's right. Well, we won't see you till we come for you, then!"

"All right," laughed Astrid, as they left. "Good-by, till then!"

CHAPTER V

THE ESCAPE FROM THRANDHEIM

THAT NIGHT the two boys watched, and discovered that their guard was changed at midnight, so they decided to make the attempt as soon as the guards were changed, as this would give them more time to get away safely.

The two succeeding days passed slowly, and the boys spent them in wandering about the town. They excited no attention, as in the harbor were one or two Danish ships, a vessel from

England, and another from Iceland, both of the latter being trading ships wintering in Norway. Sigurd could not repress a shudder as once they passed the gloomy temple of Thor.

"When will these people ever become Christian?" he said to his cousin, as they gazed at the massive stone portal. Should we really conquer Norway, let our first deed be to tear down this blood-stained old place, and erect in its stead a temple to Christ!"

"Aye," corrected Vagn. " 'If!' A vow is an easy thing, Fairhair, to make, but a hard one to fulfill. Norway has many chiefs as noble as Jarl Hakon, and no country can be conquered against its will while there is one to lead the people against the invader. King Svein, or his son Canute, may well take England, for Ethelred is a cruel and hated king; but I misdoubt that we shall ever come to Thrandheim as conquerors."

On the second evening, when Harald came to lock them in their room, he grumbled, "If it were not for you two, I would be with the Jarls now. It will soon be all up with your Jomsborgers now!"

"Why, what do you mean?" cried Vagn. "Eirik hasn't come here yet!"

"Nor will he," rejoined Harald, as he shot the bolt. "He passed outside the Firth to-day with sixty ships, and will join his father by to-morrow night at More."

"How many ships will both Jarls have?" called out Sigurd.

The man paused in the hallway. "Close onto two hundred, for Hakon took seventy-four south with him, and he will collect as many more in the south."

As the man's steps died away the two boys stared at each other in dismal silence.

"Too late, Sigurd!" Vagn's voice broke.

"Not yet," contended Sigurd, stoutly. "Ulf said that the 'Otter' was fast enough to pass Eirik, and besides, our own fleet may not have come so far north yet. Never give up!"

"That's true," granted Vagn, "for the men will probably want to land and plunder. Well, there may be hope yet."

They stood watch and watch until midnight; then, after the relieved guard had retired, Vagn nudged Sigurd and the latter emitted a long, dismal groan.

At the second groan the man outside stirred; at the third he undid the bolts, and said, "Here, what's wrong? Are you sick?"

Sigurd groaned again, muttering something, and the man entered. As he did so, Vagn threw his cloak over his head while Sigurd sprang at him. For an instant he struggled furiously, but the cloak stifled him, and soon he was lying bound on the floor, while the boys darted off down the hall.

Silently they made their way down to the women's quarters, meeting no one. The man before Astrid's door was half asleep, and they secured him with only a slight struggle. As they did so, the door opened and the girl came out, a dark cloak over her kirtle.

"Good!" she whispered, as she saw the man lying bound. "I'm all ready."

They gained the street without mishap, and ran at top speed down the hill to the harbor, without meeting a person. Arriving at the waterside, they found the "Otter's" boat awaiting them, with Ulf himself on the shore, wrapped in a cloak.

As they rowed out to the ship, Vagn told Ulf how they had escaped, and as they reached the "Otter," Ulf leaped on deck, crying in a low tone, "All ready men! Slip the cable and out oars."

The oars, already muffled, were run out, and the men soon made the "Otter" move briskly through the water, the faint starlight serving to guide them through the shipping. A little later they gained the open Firth, and the huge square sail was hoisted. They were at last on their way home!

"Well, that is the last I will see of Thrandheim for many a day," declared Ulf, as they watched the shores flit by. "It will not matter much, though. There is little to be gained in trading from this country, and next voyage I think I will go to England or Flanders. Now, don't you want to turn in? I have made the cabin ready for the Lady Astrid, and I suppose that you can turn in with the men, as I will."

By morning they were well down the coast, and as the "Otter" was a notably fast ship, Ulf had no fear of pursuit. All day they sailed south, and at evening the ship's prow was turned out to sea.

"Eirik's fleet passed down yesterday afternoon," explained Ulf, "and we do not want to run into them. If the wind holds fair we will be nearly opposite Hiorunga Firth by morning, and will turn in to the coast then."

When the boys wakened in the morning they saw that the "Otter" was indeed heading east, but a thick fog lay over the sea and the wind had dropped, the "Otter" being propelled by her oars.

"We are near the coast," declared Ulf, "and as the sun must be just rising this fog will blow away before long."

Suddenly, as they forged slowly ahead, the helmsman hailed Ulf, who sprang into the forecastle.

"Come hither, friends," he called to the boys, and pointing ahead, "what is that yonder?"

There, ahead of them, it seemed as though many lights were burning dimly through the mist. For a few minutes they gazed, puzzled; then Vagn gave a cry.

"Turn her prow, quickly!" he shouted to the helmsman. "Those are not fires at all! That is a fleet yonder, and the fog where they are must have cleared off, so that the sun shines on the gilded dragon-prows! That is what we see!"

It was too late, however, for a few minutes later the fog cleared off around them, and not a mile away they saw the high cliffs of Norway; while, farther off, gleamed the white sails of a great fleet of ships.

"Which fleet is it?" cried Sigurd, his heart leaping.

"I know not," responded Ulf. "We must run in and take our chance. If the worst comes to the worst, we can outrun them, for the wind is coming up strongly. Now for breakfast."

They ate a hurried meal, while the "Otter" plowed on swiftly through the waves. At the end of an hour, Vagn, who was watching from the forecastle, cried out in joy. "It is our own fleet! I see a sail with a red cross!"

"That is Hiorunga Firth, there to the north," declared Ulf, as Astrid joined them in the prow. "See, the fleet is heading in toward it, and we may be in time yet, for we will be up with them in half an hour."

In less than that space of time, indeed, they had come so near that they could make out the individual ships, and as they all knew Jarl Sigvald's ship by sight, Ulf steered toward that division.

What a sight it was! Ship after ship, with their gayly painted sails and glittering prows, in the shape of birds and beasts, all crowded with armed men, while, far ahead, shone the sails of more.

"That looks strange, Vagn," said Sigurd, uneasily. "I do not see any of my father's ships; it must be that he has pressed ahead, and may fall into Sigvald's trap!"

A few minutes later, the nearest ship hailed them, and as the Jomsvikings recognized Vagn and Sigurd a mighty shout went up, which rolled from ship to ship as the news spread through the fleet, and amid a roar of war-horns and clashing of arms, the "Otter" drew up to the ship of Jarl Sigvald, the oars being hastily drawn in, and Vagn leaped aboard, followed closely by Sigurd.

Sigvald was overjoyed at their escape, but there was no time for telling the story now. Vagn swiftly described the plot of Jarl Hakon, and a yell of rage arose from the men who had crowded around. It was echoed from the other ships, who had drawn in, as the helmsman shouted out the tidings.

"We have no time to lose, then," cried Sigvald, "for Bui has gone ahead and has landed men to plunder." He turned to the "Otter." "Ulf," he shouted, "keep the Lady Astrid on board, and wait for three days at the midmost of the Herey Isles, a mile or two south. If you hear no news of us by then, fly with all speed to King Svein."

Ulf waved his hand, and with a last good-by the boys parted from Astrid as the ships were cast asunder.

"I will put you on board your ship," exclaimed Sigvald to Vagn, "as we go. Up sail! Out oars!" He seized his great war-horn and blew a mighty blast. The men sprang to their places, and as they passed through the fleet cheer after cheer went up for the plucky boys who had brought the news. Hastily sails arose again and blades flashed out in the morning sun, for Bui, who had landed ahead of the fleet near Hod Island, must be warned at once.

They drew alongside Vagn's ship, and the two boys sprang on board. Vagn's men, who had followed his father and grandfather in many a hard fray, went wild at the sight of him, and greeted Sigurd no less heartily. But Fairhair was worried about his father, who he knew was over-rash, and suddenly he heard the helmsman give a great cry of dismay, and saw him wave his arms.

"What is it?" he cried, as he dashed up the ladder, followed by Vagn. But there was no need of words. There, cutting swiftly around the end of Hod Island toward Hiorunga Bay, was the division of Bui, in mad haste. He had fallen into the trap!

CHAPTER VI

HIORUNGA BAY

"FORWARD!" JARL SIGVALD'S war-horn rang out its command, and the fleet pressed on to support their rash chief. Sigurd gave a groan of dismay, but Vagn encouraged him.

"He won't be taken, Fairhair, but will return when he sees the trap. Nevertheless, we have fallen into it, for Sigvald cannot back out now with honor; we must go forward and fight like Jomsborg men!"

Bui's ships disappeared around the north end of Hod Island; then, as Sigvald got his fleet into battle array, with each half-dozen ships lashed side by side, they came back into sight, with lowered sails and oars lashing the waters to spray.

The ship of Bui was the first to reach the fleet, and as he stood in the forecastle and shouted of his discovery, Sigvald checked him, and ordered him to form his battle-line behind the fleet. Bui rowed past Vagn's ship, and as he did so Sigurd sprang on the rail, with a shout.

There was no time for stopping, so his father only waved his hand in passing, and called out, in joy and surprise, "Skoal, Sigurd! Use your best weapons to-day!" It was the last word Sigurd ever had with his father, Bui of Bornholm.

As the fleet moved forward slowly, one by one the ships of Bui straggled back and formed behind Sigvald's line. The Jomsborg men might have fled still, but they scorned to do that, and it was against their laws. The day was clouding up now, and as they turned the headland into the bay, the wind suddenly changed and blew dead against them—and there, moving on them, lay the Norse fleet!

Spreading out like a great crescent, glittering with oars and steel, Hakon's fleet moved forward, while Sigvald broke his array into three parts. Vagn Akison, by virtue of his father's place and his own renown, commanded a third part of the ships; beside his vessels lay those of Bui, while Sigvald commanded the last twenty.

"Look, Vagn!" cried Sigurd, as they watched the Norsemen, still a half-mile distant, "they are breaking up likewise!"

"Yes," replied Vagn bitterly, "but there must be nearly two hundred ships there, crowded with men. That means sixty or seventy against each of our divisions of twenty!"

Then, leaping into the waist, Vagn distributed the byrnies, or shirts of woven steel rings, and opened several chests of swords and axes, so that the men could get at them. He and Sigurd were fully armed, and naught remained but to await the attack.

It was not long in coming. Jarl Hakon's banners were suddenly raised, with a great burst of war-horns, and a flight of stones and arrows fell among the Jomsborg ships. Sigvald's banner was run up likewise, and his men replied, but the Norsemen had the advantage, for the wind was with them, and fast rising to a gale. Nevertheless, the Jomsvikings shot well, and occasioned great confusion among their foes, for their long, sharp shafts pierced shield, byrnie and body.

As the two fleets drew together, most of the bows were flung aside, and the spear-racks were emptied. Sigurd and Vagn, standing on the high forecastle with their chosen men, plied their weapons fast; but a minute later, with a crash that nearly threw them to the deck, the fleets came together.

"Concentrate on the ship against us!" shouted Sigurd, and a hail of spears poured into the large ship whose prow ground into that of Vagn's. The Norsemen strove to board, but a terrible burst of weapons met them, and an instant later Sigurd gave a cry of joy.

"Hurrah! We will win yet!" Vagn echoed the cry, for their attacker was slowly withdrawing.

"Cast a grapnel on them!" ordered Vagn, and as the Norse ship was secured he leaped into her, followed by Sigurd and his forecastle men. The Norsemen gave way, but as the Jomsvikings pressed forward a new burst of horns arose, and into the press sailed a dozen fresh ships.

"Back for your lives!" called Sigurd, as he saw a crowd of the enemy pouring aboard. "Back to our ship!"

They could see nothing of the battle on either hand, for they were surrounded by the Norse ships; but as they gained the deck of their own vessel they heard a wild shout from Bui's ships, and again the Norse line shrank backward. As Sigurd looked around, he saw Jarl Hakon's ship just behind their own.

"Look there, Vagn! Order the men to turn their spears on Hakon!"

Vagn did so, and a storm of spears and arrows poured upon the Jarl's ship. He stood proudly in the forecastle, and for a moment the rain of weapons almost hid him; then he reappeared, smiling, but his armor was ripped to pieces, and he shook himself free of it.

Now a fresh burst of foemen bore down on Vagn's division, and only the higher sides of the vikings' ships saved them. Men were falling fast, but as yet the vikings had not suffered nearly so much as had the enemy. The fighting had not yet become hand to hand, and in the thickly crowded Norse ships not a Jomsborg spear failed of its mark, and the trained skill of the vikings told heavily against the unskilled levies of Hakon.

Suddenly Sigurd laughed, and staggered. "What means the laugh, Fairhair?" called Vagn, who was directing his men in the waist.

"An arrow, but in the arm only," replied Sigurd. A shaft had pierced his arm, just above the elbow, but he snapped off the barb and drew it through the wound, and continued fighting. The next moment, however, another arrow flew past his head and was buried in the rail behind him; a third followed it, glancing from his helmet.

Sigurd realized that someone was aiming at him steadily, and marking the direction from which the arrows came, he saw the face of Thorkel Leira in one of the ships below. The man was just aiming a fourth shaft, half covered by the shield of a follower.

Catching the arrow on his shield, Sigurd flung a spear in reply, with all his force. The weapon struck full on the shield that covered Thorkel, pierced it, and Thorkel staggered back. A fresh attack drew Sigurd's attention, however, and when he looked for Thorkel again, his ship had withdrawn. Now there happened a strange and terrible thing.

The day had steadily grown darker, with a rising wind. Suddenly a blaze of lightning fell athwart the sky, and Jarl Hakon's ship stood forth in the sight of all, wrapped in lambent flame, the Jarl himself standing triumphantly in the stern, grasping a hammer like that of Thor.

A cry of horror arose from the Jomsvikings, who took the figure for that of the war god; and the lightning was followed by a thick hail, the stones as large as eggs, which burst full in the faces of the Jomsborg men.

"Thor with us! The gods fight for us!" An exultant shout pealed upward from the Norse host, who pressed onward with renewed vigor. All at once a cry broke from Vagn, a cry of anger and dismay.

"Sigurd! Look yonder!"

There behind them Jarl Sigvald had cut the lashings of his ships and was fleeing! The Jomsborg men seemed wild with terror, for now they thought that Hakon was right, that Thor and Odin were in truth fighting for him, and they lost heart.

Sigvald's ship cut through the press close behind that of Vagn, and as it passed the boy called out:

"Sigvald! Turn and fight! Turn and fight!"

But Sigvald only urged his men to greater efforts, and the sail was run up. At this Vagn seized a spear from the deck, and with a curse hurled it at the fleeing Jarl. The spear missed him, but struck down the helmsman at his side, and the ship was gone from sight in a moment.

Louder and louder pealed the war-horns of Hakon, as ship after ship followed Sigvald in his flight. Vagn's men gave one angry yell, then fought on in silence. Presently their attackers drew back for breathing-space, and as they did so the boys saw Bui's ships close at hand.

Bui was without hope, but he was true to his vows, and fought on stoutly. The Norse ships gave way before his onset, and with a shout of triumph Bui's men cut their lashings to pursue. It was a fatal error; for even as they did so, fresh Norse ships drove down on them, broke their solid front, surrounded them and began to pour in boarders.

Sigurd, watching helplessly, saw the Norsemen sweep aboard and slowly clear the deck; Bui retreated to the forecastle with a few of his men, but he was surrounded now, and his foes closed in. The old warrior fought on steadily; Sigurd caught a glimpse of his father in single combat with a gigantic Norseman, wielding an axe. Bui slipped, and the axe whirled above him and fell on his helmet, wounding him terribly; but recovering, Bui cut down his foe, then leaped to the rail.

"Overboard, all Bui's men!" rang out his voice, loudly. Just then the fight closed in on Vagn afresh, but Sigurd caught a flash of armor, and knew that his father had died as a viking should, beneath the waves.

The Jomsborg ships broke up now, each fighting desperately to the last. One by one they were boarded and swept clean of men, and at length it came the turn of Vagn's ship.

Then, as the Norsemen swept over the side, the vikings put sword and axe in play for the first time, the boys at their head. Time after time the flood poured across the bulwarks, and time after time the Jomsborg steel stemmed the tide and drove it back. At last a wild yell arose behind them, and those of the crew who were left retreated slowly to the forecastle, fighting desperately.

A very handsome man, of lofty stature, swept over the prow with his men, and cut his way to Vagn. The two met with a clash of swords, and the tall man, evidently a leader of note, fell beneath Vagn's blows; he was up again, however, and his men swiftly closed around Vagn. Sigurd gave a shout of rage, and sprang to his friend's side, but too late.

The sea of fierce faces swept down on him, but recoiled before the Jomsborg axes. Vagn lay motionless, and Sigurd, bestriding his body, faced the handsome leader, axe in hand. The other's sword flashed, and for a moment Sigurd was hard put to it to ward off the storm of blows; then his axe fell on the other's helm, and the man staggered back. Before he could follow up his advantage, Sigurd slipped in a pool of blood—he saw a sword whirled above him, gave his battle-cry once more—and sank across the body of Vagn.

With the fall of Vagn and Sigurd, the battle was over. Thirty-five ships had fled with Sigvald, twenty-five had remained with Bui and Vagn. One by one they were boarded and cleared, for Jarl Hakon gave no quarter; one by one they floated out of the whirl, empty but for dying and dead. The vikings died beneath sword and spear, or followed Bui's example and plunged beneath the waves, while far in the distance the white sails of Sigvald glittered awhile and then vanished to the south.

CHAPTER VII

HOW VAGN KEPT HIS VOW

"THAT IS all, I think; twenty of them. No, this one stirred somewhat. Here, lift him up."

Sigurd opened his eyes. Over him were bending two men, one his handsome opponent, the other—Thorkel Leira. The boy struggled to his feet, the former assisting.

It was only mid-afternoon, the storm had passed, and about the Jomsborg ships lay the Norse fleet. Glancing around, Sigurd saw the decks heaped with dead, and in the waist of the ship was a little group of Jomsvikings, their arms bound. Then he remembered Vagn.

Thorkel Leira was holding a horn of water to Vagn's lips, and as Sigurd, weak and dizzy, knelt at his friend's side, he wondered why Thorkel thus aided his deadly enemy. He was soon to know.

Vagn looked up. As he caught sight of Thorkel he dashed the horn aside and struggled up on Sigurd's arm. Before he could speak, however, a group of men approached and bound the boys' arms, under the orders of the handsome chief. Then they were led into the waist of the ship and joined the others.

The men gave a murmur of joy. "It was a noble fight, eh, Vagn?" muttered an old viking, Biorn of Bretland, or Wales. "I have fought for twenty years under your father Aki and your grandfather Palnatoki, and I never saw a greater battle than this."

"It is a sad one for the brotherhood, Biorn," replied Vagn weakly, "when the Jarl himself turned tail and fled."

A murmur of anger ran around the group, then Sigurd asked, "Who is the tall man, and what will they do with us?"

Biorn nodded toward some small boats near by. "They are taking us on shore, I know not why. Neither do I know the man."

A group of Norsemen approached, and the captives were led to the boats, which were swiftly rowed to the shore. Here, upon a long fallen tree, sat the Jomsborg men, with their feet bound in a long rope; but their hands were left free.

The Norsemen surrounded them, binding up wounds, exchanging rough jests on the battle, and examining with awe and wonder these vikings whose name was so famous, and who had fought so stoutly against such great odds.

Presently the tall man and Thorkel Leira landed. "I have it, Sigurd!" cried Vagn. "That handsome man must be Jarl Eirik, Hakon's son!"

At that instant the handsome man came up to the captives.

"Never mind, we will soon be back again with good Queen Gunhild."

"You fought well and stoutly, Jomsvikings," he said, "and I am in truth sorry that Jarl Hakon has ordered that no quarter be given, for I would fain spare your lives if I might."

"It is the fortune of war," replied Vagn, smiling bravely. "Had we conquered, I do not think that Sigvald would have spared Hakon either, yet Christian men have more merciful customs than you who follow Thor and Odin."

The other flushed slightly, turning to Thorkel. “It is not to my taste, Thorkel, to slay these helpless men thus.”

Thorkel smiled his cunning, cruel smile. “It is much to my taste, Jarl, to slay Vagn Akison!”

At this Vagn cried out, “Yet you feared to stand before me in battle, Thorkel! Say, will you loose my bonds and meet me now with sword or axe?”

A murmur of assent arose from the Norsemen who stood around, but Thorkel shook his head, as he fingered the big axe in his hand.

As Thorkel withdrew to speak with the handsome man for a moment, old Biorn leaned over and whispered excitedly to Sigurd: “It is just a chance, Fairhair, so try it.”

Sigurd nodded as Thorkel returned. “Best begin with the chiefs, Thorkel,” he cried, although his heart beat madly, for if Biorn’s plan did not work nothing could save his life. Thorkel advanced and stood in front of him.

“Since you are in haste to die, let it be so.”

“Wait!” exclaimed Sigurd, as the man swung his axe aloft. “Let someone hold my hair, lest it be defiled and soiled.”

A Norseman, with a word of admiration at the lad’s bravery, stepped forward and gathered up the boy’s long, fair hair in his hands, and the axe swung.

As it descended, Sigurd jerked his body so strongly to one side that the axe was buried in the earth, and Thorkel lost his balance and fell forward. A laugh went up from the crowd as the angry man rose, but the handsome chief advanced and held his arm.

“Who are you, handsome lad?”

“I am called Sigurd, and am Bui’s son,” replied Sigurd, looking up to the other’s eyes, which met his in admiration. “The Jomsborg men are not yet all dead!”

“Truly you are a son of Bui!” exclaimed the other. “Will you take life and peace from me?”

“If you have the power to give it,” answered Sigurd.

The man drew himself up. "He offers who has power to give—Jarl Eirik Hakonson."

"Thanks, Jarl," replied Sigurd, with a breath of relief, "I will accept it." The whisper of old Biorn had proved true.

Thorkel, with a dark frown, plucked up his axe, and cried angrily, "Though you spare all these men, Eirik, Vagn shall not escape me!"

With that he raised the axe. As the weapon whirled, Biorn flung himself against Thorkel's knees. The man stumbled, the axe fell; and Vagn, springing up in a flash, seized it and fulfilled his vow.

A great shout of applause rang out, for above all things Norsemen love a brave deed. They crowded around admiringly, and Jarl Eirik with a smile, said, "Will you also take life, Vagn?"

"That I will," answered Vagn, "if you will also give it to my men as well."

"Loose them from the rope," commanded the Jarl, and it was done.

By this time evening was coming on, and the Norsemen hastily made a camp on the shore; Jarl Hakon was encamped across the bay. The men sat around the fires and talked in low tones, and presently the two boys were summoned to the fire of the Jarl.

Eirik greeted them with a winning smile. "Sit down and eat, friends, for I have somewhat to think over. My father gave express commands that no Jomsviking was to be spared; why I gave you life I know not, save that you were but boys, and full of courage. Now, whither would you go?"

Vagn looked at Sigurd. The latter nodded, and Vagn told Eirik the story of Ulf and Astrid, who were waiting a few miles away. When he finished, the Jarl sat in thought for a moment.

"Here is my counsel. If I send you both off together, my father will send a ship after you to slay you, and I will not have my promise broken. I go home from here by land to the mountains, and so to my own earldom. I would advise that you, Vagn, come with me, for I can protect you, and let Sigurd rejoin Ulf with the eighteen Jomsvikings who are left. I will send you home, Vagn, within a month at most."

"That is a good plan," exclaimed Vagn. "Do you not think so, Fairhair?"

Sigurd assented, though he disliked to part with his cousin; but there was no help for it, and so it was decided.

Early the next morning the Jomsborg men and Sigurd ran out three small boats and said farewell to Vagn. Eirik armed them all well, and made them many presents; and as they pushed off Vagn stood on the shore, waving farewell.

"I'll see you at Jomsborg next month," called Sigurd. "Farewell!"

Under a fair wind the three boats ran quickly down the bay, rounded the end of Hod Island, and arrived in an hour at the Herey Islands. Steering in between the largest and smallest, they reached into the bay, and there before them lay the "Otter." A shout of greeting came to them, and as they pulled up to the side Ulf Ringsson sprang on the rail.

"What news of the battle? Who won?"

Sigurd pointed to his men, all of them wounded. "These are all left of the Jomsvikings," he replied. A cry of horror went up, and Ulf staggered back.

"Impossible! Where is your father Bui, Jarl Sigvald, Vagn Akison, Aslak Holmskalle? They cannot be dead!"

"Some are even worse off," said Sigurd, climbing the rail wearily. "Vagn is safe, my father is dead with Aslak, and Sigvald and his men have fled home again."

While Astrid greeted Sigurd, and his wounded and weary men clambered on board, Ulf remained stunned with amazement. "Fled! Fled!" he muttered. "The Jarl himself false to his vows!"

He could not believe it; for it was the most sacred law of Jomsborg that no viking should turn his back to a foe. Sigurd told of the fight, while the excited sailors questioned his men, and as he finished Astrid sprang forward.

"You are wounded, Sigurd! See, your arm is all red, and your head is bloody!"

"Yes, bind it up," laughed Sigurd bitterly, "for the Jomsborg rules are shattered with the brotherhood forever!" Then he reeled, and would have fallen save for the strong hand of Ulf.

They carried him to the cabin, and while the men set sail, Ulf, who was skilled as a leech, extracted the broken arrow-head and bound up the wound. The other, on his head, was not dangerous, and Sigurd soon fell into a deep sleep, not waking till the afternoon.

The rocking of the ship told him that they were out at sea, so he hastened on deck; to his surprise, the land was out of sight, and a heavy gale was blowing.

"So you are awake!" cried Astrid. "How do you feel?"

"Ready for another battle," laughed Sigurd, then his brow clouded over as he thought of his father. Astrid, divining his thoughts, was silent for a moment, then changed the subject.

"We had no sooner left the land than this gale broke on us, and Ulf says that it is growing stronger every minute."

Sigurd looked around. Indeed, the gale was a heavy north-easter, and now he noticed that the sail was close-reefed, and that everything was stowed away save the three boats in which he had come to the "Otter," which were lashed securely in the shelter of the high stern.

"Hello, I'm glad to see you around so soon!" cried Ulf cheerily, and the boy gripped his hand in thanks.

"If Jarl Hakon were here, Ulf, he would say that Ran, the ocean queen, was trying to complete the work begun by Thor and Odin at Hiorunga Bay."

Sigurd smiled at Astrid, but the captain looked about anxiously.

"We are in for a bad blow, Sigurd. It is good that the 'Otter' is stanch, for to tell you the truth, we are far from our course for Denmark, and it may well be that we shall be driven farther still."

CHAPTER VIII

"SKOAL, TO KING OLAF!"

MUCH AS they loved the keen wind and dash of the spray, Sigurd and Astrid were soon driven from their post in the bow of the "Otter," for the seas began rolling up tremendously, and they were forced to seek the shelter of the cabin. The men were all stowed away below, save for the watch on duty, and as the "Otter" was a stanch vessel, and Ulf a good captain, Sigurd had no fear but that they would outride the storm safely.

"How strange it all seems!" remarked Astrid that evening. "Only a few short weeks ago we were all together at the heirship feast of my uncle, and now the Jomsborg power is shattered, Vagn is far off in Norway, and here we are driving no one knows where, over the sea! I wonder what became of your falcon!"

Sigurd laughed. "I wonder what! Never mind, we will soon be back again with good Queen Gunhild. Hello! how goes it, Ulf?"

The captain entered, dripping with brine, and shook his head. "Badly, Sigurd. It is fully the worst storm I ever saw, and I was a fool for ever putting to sea at this time of year. However, we must trust in God and do our best to weather it."

So for five days the "Otter" scudded before the gale, utterly helpless. There was plenty of work for all, however, for the giant seas swept the low hull repeatedly, and everyone was kept busy bailing the ship, from morning to night. It was lucky, indeed, that the eighteen Jomsvikings had come aboard with Sigurd, for as it was all were so exhausted by the constant labor that they worked mechanically, and at the end of every watch they lashed themselves to the bulwarks and dropped to sleep at once.

On the fifth evening Sigurd was sitting in the cabin, talking to Astrid, when they were startled by a loud crash, followed by shouts and cries. Sigurd ran out on deck.

"The mast!" shouted Ulf in his ear. Sigurd turned and saw only a ragged stump. Ulf motioned him inside, for the gale blew all words away, and when the door was closed cried in despair,

"Sigurd, I have done my best! Had the mast held we would have been safe, for the storm is breaking, I think; but an hour since I saw land in the west, and we cannot beat off now."

"Know you what land it was?" inquired Astrid. Ulf shook his head despondently.

"For aught I know, it may be Scotland, or the Fareys, or the Orkneys, or even that Vinland which the Icelanders say Eirik the Red discovered. I am lost, and we are in the hands of God."

Presently Ulf went out again, and managed to rig enough canvas to the stump of the mast to keep the "Otter's" head before the wind. In this fashion they drove ahead all night, and with daybreak a long line of cliffs was disclosed, straight ahead, and only a few miles away.

As they stood watching on the forecastle, Astrid pulled at Sigurd's arm. "Why can't we escape in those boats, when the 'Otter' drives ashore?" she shouted in his ear, pointing to the three boats lashed in the stern. This had not occurred to Sigurd or Ulf, because the viking ships themselves were so small that they rarely carried boats, as they could be drawn up on shore easily enough.

"Hurrah! Good idea, Astrid!" Sigurd hastened to Ulf's side, but the latter shrugged his shoulders at the plan.

"To what end? We will only be putting off death for a few minutes; once we drive on those cliffs and it will be over."

Nevertheless, at Sigurd's urging the boats were made ready, for although the storm was breaking they were fast nearing the shore. Into each boat were put arms and food, well secured.

"We must leave before she strikes," shouted Ulf, "else the seas will sweep boats and all away."

Sigurd nodded, and returned to Astrid. The cliffs were not a mile away now, and they could see the white spray flying high from the dark rocks. Presently Ulf motioned to them, and they descended into the waist of the ship, joining the crowd about the boats. Sigurd took command of one, Ulf of another, and Biorn of Bretland commanded the third; then all awaited the word. The "Otter" was low in the water now, and it would be no great task to launch the boats over her side.

Presently Ulf gave a sharp command. "Out!" The six men assigned to each boat lifted it, poised it an instant on the rail, then as a giant crest foamed along the three boats were borne out together. A man leaped in each, and fended off from the "Otter's" side with a spear, while the rest hastily embarked.

"Farewell, old Otter!" cried Ulf, the last to leave; and as they swept from the vessel they saw her suddenly lurch and reel wildly.

"Just in time!" said Sigurd to Astrid, who was in his boat. "She struck then, but scraped over; next time—"

While he was speaking, the ship heeled far over on her side, amid a cloud of flying foam; but they could not watch her further, for now they were fighting for their own lives. Sigurd was at the tiller, and he followed Ulf closely, while the men rowed steadily. The seas swept them in under the cliffs, and Ulf suddenly raised his hand and waved it. Straight at the high walls his boat darted, and then Sigurd saw a little stretch of beach before them as he swept in.

With a last stroke the men drove the boats up, then leaped out and drew them up. Sigurd carried Astrid up the beach and looked around. The cliffs did not seem so steep now, and Sigurd realized that they would be able to climb them, just as Ulf joined him. The captain was in more hopeful spirits now.

"Your plan certainly saved us, lady," he exclaimed to Astrid. "I had given up hope—strange I did not think of those boats myself. But we so seldom use small boats that I never gave them a thought. Now, Fairhair, what had we best do?"

Sigurd looked out to sea, where the hull of the "Otter" was fast breaking up under the smashing blows of the waves. "Well, I think we had better take the arms and food from the boats, scale those cliffs, and see where we are. We have over a score of well-armed men, and the folk, whoever they are, will hesitate before molesting us."

Ulf turned and gave the necessary orders, then, followed by Biorn and the rest, they made for the cliffs. These, as Sigurd had foreseen, offered no great difficulties to the Norsemen, who were all used to climbing about their native fiords, and in half an hour they stood on the brow and looked about.

Before them lay a heavily wooded country, rolling with small hills and valleys, but without a sign of habitation. The storm was nearly over now, and while the seas still rolled mountain-high below them, the sun was just breaking through the clouds, and in the distance they caught the sheen of a river. The men hailed the sun with a cry of delight, and Ulf pointed to the river.

"Let us make for that, Sigurd, and there we can have fresh water and a meal. After that we can decide what to do."

So, striking away from the sea, they entered the forest. It was the end of autumn now, and though the leaves had fallen from many of the trees, the forest was composed in great part of pines, fresh and green. Even Biorn looked puzzled as he tried to make out the country.

"I do not think it is Scotland," he said, "and certainly it is neither the Fareys nor the Orkneys. It is not my own land of Wales, for that was far from our course; it might be Ireland, but I have never been in that land."

"Ireland!" cried Astrid. "Why, isn't that where men say Olaf Tryggveson is king?"

"So it is," rejoined Sigurd, "but it must be a wide land, and we have small hope of finding Northmen here."

"Well," remarked Ulf, "we can but push on boldly. If we are indeed in Ireland, we are lucky, for men say that in that country there is the finest civilization in Europe—"

"There used to be, Ulf," growled old Biorn, "just as there used to be in Wales, my own land; but the heathen vikings have well-nigh destroyed it all."

Soon they come out on the banks of a wide and sluggish river, and with cries of joy the men rushed down to the bank and plunged in, drinking greedily and washing the salt brine from their bodies. Sigurd filled a horn for Astrid, but as she returned it a shout broke from Biorn:

"Back! Back! Out swords, men!"

At the same moment a flight of arrows fell among the men, striking down two of the sailors, and a wild yell reechoed from the trees. The Jomsvikings, protected by their byrnies and helmets, hastily scrambled up the bank and fell into line around the leaders, the others forming behind them.

Dark forms flitted among the trees, and Sigurd called out, "Shield to shield, men! Hold your spears ready for the word."

The vikings' bows were useless, the strings having been soaked, so they waited helplessly. Arrows fell thickly, but Sigurd covered Astrid with his shield, and they did no further harm. Then, with a yell, a crowd of men broke out of the forest; they were clad in woolen tunics, a few wore armor, while all held spears and axes. As they charged, Sigurd gave the word.

The attackers broke as the heavy Jomsborg spears sent half a dozen to the ground; but as they did so a war-horn rang out behind them, and a voice cried in Norse, "At them, men! For the Cross!"

Through the forest glades swept a band of steel-clad men, driving the others before them in headlong flight. As pursuers and pursued vanished amid the trees, their leader approached the little band of shipwrecked men.

Although Sigurd was tall, he noted with surprise that this man was a good head and shoulders above him, and broad in proportion. His features were frank and open, his eyes blue and piercing, and his hair was red-gold, waving over his golden armor. He wore a blue cloak, a gold helm and gold-linked byrnie, and on his shield was a great cross in red.

"Are you Christian men?" he asked, as he drew near, fixing his eyes on Sigurd.

"That we are," cried the latter, joyfully. "Where are we? Who are you who rescued us so opportunely?"

"You are on the coast of Ireland, and my city of Dublin is only three miles distant. These Irish would never have dared come so near had they not thought me absent from home on a cruise. I am Olaf, son of King Tryggve of Norway."

At this the Jomsvikings gazed in wonder on the handsome chief; then with a blast on his war-horn old Biorn led the shout: "Skoal to King Olaf! Skoal!"

CHAPTER IX

HOW ASTRID FARED FORTH

"THANKS, FRIENDS!" smiled Olaf, and Sigurd thought that never in all his life had he seen so handsome and kingly a man. "Who are you, young sir? And who are these men? Truly, I have seldom beheld so fine a set of warriors, wounded though they are!"

"I am Sigurd Buisson of Bornholm, King, and with me is Astrid of Vendland, niece of Gunhild of Denmark. This is Ulf Ringsson, captain of our ship, and as for my men, they are the last of the Jomsvikings."

"What!" Olaf's eyes opened in amazement, and he threw down his weapons. "Tell me your tale, quickly! I heard of Svein's accession feast, but nothing of what followed. Has Sigvald, then, won Norway?"

Sigurd told of the battle at Hiorunga Bay, and Olaf's face darkened. As he concluded, the Norsemen of Olaf returned and all took up the march for Dublin, Sigurd's men mingling with the others.

While they walked along Olaf told them of how he had fled to Russia when his father was murdered, how he had become a viking, wandering the ocean, and how he had been baptized. Then he had come to Ireland and won the kingdom of Dublin, ruling it together with his brother-in-law, Olaf Kvaran.

"We saw your ship from the castle," he explained, "so I came out to aid any who might escape. Now, what do you intend doing?"

"As to that," returned Sigurd, "I care little; but the Lady Astrid here must be returned home."

"Then will you be my man?" inquired Olaf.

"That will I!" Sigurd turned to his men and called, "Listen, Jomsvikings! What say you to taking service with King Olaf?"

"Aye!" the shout went up, with clashing of arms, and Olaf smiled. "That pleases me well, Sigurd, for a few Jomsborg men are worth a hundred others. As to Astrid, she must take her chance; it is too late in the season for ships now, and I fear she must remain with us till spring. However, that can wait; there is the city."

As they left a valley, Dublin lay before them, and the Jomsborg men cried out in surprise, for the town was very beautiful, and defended with strong walls and towers such as they had seldom seen. Soon they were riding through the streets, and the men were quartered in the palace, where Olaf also assigned rooms to Ulf, Sigurd and Astrid.

Olaf sent fresh and new garments to all, and soon they rejoined him in the great hall for the midday meal. Here Olaf introduced them to Queen Gyda, his brother-in-law, and one or two of his chief men, and soon they were all chatting away merrily, forgetful of their past troubles.

After the meal Sigurd led his Jomsborg men into the hall, up to the high seat of Olaf. Kneeling, Sigurd placed his hands between those of the King, and swore to obey him and to be his man. One by one the rest followed his example, and when the ceremony was over Olaf presented each man with a shield, ornamented with a large red cross; but to Sigurd he gave a magnificent golden helmet, on top of which was wrought a dragon in the same metal, its wings outstretched and sweeping far back.

"I won this helm in Russia," smiled the King, "so see that the dragon bears his face ever toward my foes!"

Sigurd was overjoyed with the gift, which was a helm worthy a king, and thanked Olaf most sincerely. The next day he was given a command in the courtmen, or bodyguard, and took up his new duties.

A week later the first snow fell, but as Astrid had given up all hope of reaching home before spring, she did not mind greatly. Indeed, Olaf's court was a pleasant one, and both Sigurd and Astrid enjoyed themselves immensely.

Queen Gyda became very fond of Astrid, who was a favorite with all because of her sunny disposition and gay heart. Sigurd's wound soon healed, and by Yuletide both had adjusted themselves to their new surroundings.

Sigurd grew much attached to King Olaf. Olaf was high-tempered, but just, and in warlike exercises no one could equal him. Often he would go down to the harbor, bid his men row out a warship, and then while the oars were out walk along them. Not content with this, he would sometimes juggle knives or balls, keeping his balance perfectly.

He took great interest in "Fairhair," for Sigurd's nickname could not be left behind, and himself added to the store of sword-tricks the boy had learned in the school at Jomsborg.

Yuletide passed, and a few weeks later a ship drove into the bay, to the astonishment of everyone, for the ships of that day did not often venture on voyages in winter. The new arrivals were from Norway, and were traders.

It happened that Ulf had not heard of the ship, and as he sat at meat that evening he leaped to his feet suddenly.

"What is that man who just passed the door?" he exclaimed. The King darted a swift, keen look at the captain, and replied: "That is Thorir Klakke, who arrived to-day from Norway with his brother Ketil, bearing news and goods for trading."

"Then beware of him, Olaf," remarked Ulf, "for I have often seen him in deep converse with Jarl Hakon. He is here for no good, I think."

Shortly after this, Thorir and his brother entered. Both men were short, dark, and well dressed; but their eyes roved about constantly beneath their low brows. Ketil's face in particular was powerful, yet sullen.

Thorir started slightly at sight of Sigurd, but Olaf greeted him kindly, and he sat down silently, falling into low converse with his brother. For several days nothing occurred, save that Thorir had frequent audiences with Olaf; but at every meal Sigurd noted Ketil's gaze fixed on himself or Astrid, although it dropped before that of Sigurd. This puzzled him, for he could not see why Ketil should be interested, and it also angered him, for he saw plainly that Astrid did not like it.

A week or two after the arrival of the Norsemen, Olaf and Sigurd were talking together, while Astrid and the Queen were busy with their sewing. Suddenly the King exclaimed, abruptly:

"Sigurd, how would you like to visit Norway next summer?"

The boy started, meeting the King's eye eagerly. "Nothing better, my lord!"

Olaf smiled. "Well, Thorir urges me to take the realm of Norway from Hakon, as is my right. He says that the bonders are not satisfied with the Jarl's rule and that it would be an easy task to overthrow him. What think you?"

"Well," responded Sigurd, "if Jarl Hakon could overthrow the might of Jomsborg, methinks it would go hard with others who attempt his kingdom."

Here Astrid, who had been listening earnestly, broke in: "Perhaps, King Olaf, Hakon might have sent this man to bring you into his power!"

Olaf stared at Astrid for a moment, then his blue eyes lit up with a fierce light, and his fist came down on the table. "As I am a Christian man, that is it! Beware, Thorir Klakke! If I go to Norway, it will not be as your master expects!"

"Hakon has sixteen Jarls under him," remarked the Queen, "and some of them may not be such great friends of his by next fall. If each commands one of the districts of the kingdom, you may find an opening in that way, Olaf."

The King nodded. "In any case, I will take a strong force. And when I do rule Norway, I swear by this sword that I will root out paganism from the land, and bring the country under the Cross of the white Christ! The Hammer of Thor shall vanish from the land!"

For a moment the King's handsome face was stern, and filled with a high resolve; then it softened again, as he rose and bid Sigurd good-night.

A few days later the boy felt the bearing of Ketil becoming intolerable, and he resolved to warn the man to gaze at Astrid less insolently. It was his watch upon the walls that night, and as he was passing through the narrow and dark streets, three men sprang out on him, from a doorway. Although taken by surprise, Sigurd put his back to a wall, and drew his sword.

His light shield cracked and split under the furious blows, although the men could only attack Sigurd singly, for a doorway on either side of him afforded some protection. Knowing that his men were not far, Sigurd shouted the old Jomsborg call, and at this the three assailants redoubled their efforts.

Sigurd caught an axe blow on his shield, which sheared it from his arm; but his sword fell upon the other's shoulder, and with a muttered curse the axe fell. Springing out, Sigurd clove the helm of the second man with one quick stroke, but he received at the same time a tremendous blow from the sword of the third man. The boy staggered, and fell over the body of the man he had killed; and a loud shout came from the corner, with torches streaming in the lane, which put the assassins to flight.

The men gave a shout of anger as they saw Sigurd lying in the street, but the men had escaped, and Biorn raised Sigurd tenderly. The latter, thanks to the gift of Olaf, was unhurt, but a dent in the side of the helmet bore witness to the blow's power.

Biorn turned over the body of the slain man, and the men gave a cry. "He is one of the crew of Thorir Klakke! To the King!"

"Stop!" shouted Sigurd as the vikings were rushing off. "Let this wait till morning; they cannot escape, and the King dislikes to be disturbed from his sleep."

They yielded, although unwillingly, and Sigurd took up his guard again. This was to be an eventful night, however, for two hours after midnight one of the harbor guards ran up to him, and cried:

"Sigurd, Thorir Klakke's ship is leaving, and will not answer our signals; come quickly!"

Calling to Biorn, Sigurd ran down to the harbor, and in the dim light could see the trading vessel, which had not been drawn up on shore, slowly making her way toward the harbor entrance, for the port was too wide to freeze far from shore.

Without wasting time in hailing, Sigurd sprang into a light skiff, moored at the edge of the ice, set a dozen men at the oars, and in five minutes was close to the ship.

"Way enough, men," he said, then lifted his voice: "What business have you leaving Dublin thus? Come back and give an accounting!"

At this the oars flashed out the faster, and a mocking voice responded: "What, indeed, young cockerel? Go back to Jomsborg and—"

"Help, Sigurd! Help!" broke in a cry, " they have—"

Silence fell again, but something flashed into the water beside Sigurd's boat, and as Biorn picked it up, the boy exclaimed:

"That was Astrid's voice! Alongside, men!"

Only a mocking laugh answered, as the square sail rose and the ship filled away. "No use," said Biorn. "Better return; see, I have picked this up." He held out something to Sigurd.

Now Sigurd and Astrid both knew the secret of Runic writing, which only the priests and high chieftains among the Northmen were familiar with; and looking down at the object, Sigurd saw it was a bit of wood, with something scratched on it. The light was too dim to see further.

"Back to the landing!" cried Sigurd, a terrible fear in his heart. "Hasten!"

As they drew ashore he leaped out, and held the piece of wood up to the light of a torch.

CHAPTER X

FAREWELL TO DUBLIN

BIORN AND the vikings crowded around, as he deciphered the scratches, for they were unable to read Runic, which was more like shorthand than anything else. A cry of dismay burst from Sigurd.

"Listen, men! 'Ketil bears me to England! Rescue, Sigurd!' Come, men, to the palace!"

"To the palace! To the palace!" They echoed his words, and the terrible Jomsborg battle-yell startled the sleeping town, and pealed up to the castle.

"Bring Thorir Klakke, but harm him not," commanded Sigurd, "while I arouse the king."

Olaf, however, was already up, wakened by the tumult. Sword in hand, he entered the great hall just as Sigurd burst in at the other end.

"What means this uproar?" roared Olaf, his eyes blazing with anger.

"Justice and vengeance, King!" panted Sigurd, as he handed Olaf the bit of wood. Sheathing his weapon with a frown, Olaf took the object, and by the light of the torches read the message.

"What means it?"

"Astrid of Vendland is kidnaped, Olaf, and I was set upon by three men in the streets. One I killed, and he was a man of Thorir Klakke's—stay, here is Thorir now."

Biorn and two vikings entered the hall behind Sigurd, leading the terrified Thorir. Olaf, grasping the whole situation, strode up and thundered in the merchant's ear:

"What means this night's work? Where is your brother?"

Thorir stammered out, "Indeed, my lord, I know not. Is he not in his rooms?" Then, growing bolder, "Am I accountable for Ketil's doings, Olaf? What mean you?"

Olaf looked into the man's eyes a moment, and before that terrible gaze Thorir squirmed helplessly, but did not weaken. "Begone to your rooms!" said the King, contemptuously, and turned abruptly to Sigurd.

"Now tell me the tale in full."

Sigurd told him of the attack, of the flight of the ship, and of Astrid's cry, in a few words. "I sent men to her rooms," he concluded. "Here they come now."

Close on his words the men entered, with them Queen Gyda and some of her ladies. Queen Gyda, who had learned the cause of the tumult from the vikings, told how a messenger had summoned Astrid an hour before, saying that Sigurd was hurt in a brawl, and how the girl had run out hastily.

"Come with me, quickly," ordered the King, and Sigurd followed him to the ramparts of the castle. The dawn was just breaking, and far out at sea they saw a speck of white.

"With Thorir I will deal later, for we have no proof against him as yet," said the King, "but that man yonder has dishonored me, and shall die. Fairhair, take what men you will from my courtmen, and the 'Crane,' the fastest longship in the harbor. Ketel has taken his brother's ship, so you should soon come up with him. The 'Crane' is in the water, and is well provisioned; so hasten—be off within the hour."

"Thanks, Olaf!" replied Sigurd. "I was about to ask this very thing of you. I will take my own men and thirty of yours. Thanks, for all your kindness, and above all for your friendship, Olaf!"

The King smiled sadly. "I have few friends, Sigurd, and methinks you are the most faithful of them, though the newest. No, go with God, and forget him not, for it is still the season of storms."

As Sigurd turned away, the King stopped him with a sudden impulse.

"Stay! Give me your hands." Wondering, Sigurd put his hands between Olaf's. "Now swear again your oath to me, Jarl Sigurd!"

The boy, overcome by this unexpected title and honor, stumbled through the oath, and rose with tears in his eyes.

"I need no oath to be faithful, King Olaf! When you have won Norway, the title of friend is all I want."

Quick tears sprang to Olaf's eyes also, and unbuckling his sword-belt, he threw it over Sigurd's shoulders, saying, "I have no earldoms yet, but here is my Jarl-gift, my friend. Farewell!"

Sigurd wrung the King's hand, then turned and ran down the stairway to the courtyard. Hastily assembling his men, and choosing thirty from Olaf's followers, he sent them down to the "Crane" with Biorn, and followed them himself a few minutes later, after bidding Ulf farewell. The captain would have accompanied him, but Olaf was sending him on a mission to an Irish king in the interior.

The "Crane," as Olaf had said, was well stocked with all things needful for a voyage; so, weighing anchor, the sail was run up and the voyage begun. As they left the harbor, Sigurd told his men of his advancement, and it was greeted with a shout of satisfaction; for the Jomsvikings were proud of their young leader, and the other men had heard many tales of his bravery. Indeed, even though the title carried no lands, it was the ambition of every chief of good birth to be made Jarl, or Earl, for the Jarls were second only to the King.

The oars were run out, for the wind was light, and under all speed the "Crane" ran southward. Ketil's ship was out of sight, but his goal was known, and Sigurd was confident that he would overtake the other ship before night.

"Why, think you, is he heading for England instead of for Norway?" Sigurd asked old Biorn.

The latter paused a moment. "Well, Jarl Sigurd, it is in my mind that Ketil is a cunning man. If he took Astrid to Norway, he would make nothing; but by taking her to England, much. King Ethelred would pay high for such a hostage from King Svein of Denmark."

"Oh, I see! Then she will not be harmed?"

"Assuredly not, Jarl, at least till she reaches England, which I trust will never be. Ethelred is as treacherous as Hakon himself, and if she once falls into his clutches it would be a bad business."

They did not come up with Ketil's ship so soon as Sigurd expected, for not till midafternoon did the helmsman give a shout, and Sigurd, running to the forecastle, saw a white speck far ahead.

"Lower the sail," he ordered, "and get out all the oars," for until then only half the oars had been going, to save the men's strength. "We cannot come up with them to-day," he explained, "so it were best to let Ketil think himself safe."

So the sail was lowered and the "Crane" proceeded under her oars till nightfall, when the sail was hoisted again and the oars taken in. The wind freshened toward midnight, when Sigurd relinquished the watch to Biorn, and at dawn he was aroused by the old viking.

"Come, Jarl! A squall from the west has broken on us, and it is daybreak." Sigurd followed him to the deck. There he found the sail close-reefed, and the "Crane" running before a squall of wind and driving snow. There was nothing to be done, however, save to await the sunrise.

As full day broke, but dark and gloomy, with flurries of snow, a shout went up, for not half a mile distant lay Ketil's ship, also running before the wind.

"Shake out the reefs, men! We may as well take chances, and make sure of her."

Biorn stopped him, however, and pointing ahead, showed Sigurd a dull gray line. "England, Jarl, or Wales, rather! It would be useless to try to board Ketil in this heavy sea; the ships would be smashed to kindling-wood."

Sigurd reluctantly acknowledged that the old viking was right, so he contented himself with following the other ship, while with every hour the Welsh coast grew plainer ahead of them. The sky cleared off, but the sea was still running too high for any attempt at boarding.

"I know where we are, Jarl," called out the helmsman. "Do you remember that great headland, Biorn?"

"That I do," exclaimed the viking. "See how the coast falls away there, Sigurd? That is Wales, where live my own people, and we are entering a great firth which goes far up into the country, and on the right is the Saxon kingdom of Wessex. I recall it well. Six years ago we sailed up and plundered a town they call Bristol. It must be that Ketil means to land along the Saxon coast."

Sigurd gazed with interest on the lofty cliffs, but soon they turned the last headland, and Ketil pointed his ship due east. Sigurd saw that they were indeed in a great firth; the "Crane" easily held her own with the fleeing ship, but did not approach closer.

"If they succeed in getting ashore, whither would they take the Lady Astrid, think you?" inquired Sigurd.

"To King Ethelred, doubtless," answered Biorn, "at London, in the east. However, they cannot escape us now."

"Arm yourselves, men!" ordered Sigurd, a little later, "the sea is falling fast, and we will run aboard."

Ketil, however, saw this also, and evidently resolved to take no chances, for he turned in toward the coast, plying his oars desperately. The two ships, a quarter of a mile apart, drew into the coast and ran along the low shores.

Suddenly Biorn gave a cry of fury. "He will escape us yet!" Ketil's ship, just beyond a headland, was turned in toward the shore. The helmsman turned the "Crane" and the sail was run down as the other ship disappeared. Under all her oars, the "Crane" darted ahead, and there before them lay the ship of Ketil, while the crew were leaping out. A band of armed men from the town above ran down and met Ketil.

Sigurd did not wait to see the meeting, but as the "Crane" scraped on the sand and ice he leaped overboard, followed by Biorn, and waded ashore. Amid Ketil's party Sigurd had seen the flutter of a dress, and he knew there was little use searching the other ship, so he dashed up the hill. Suddenly, however, a flight of arrows fell among Sigurd's men, and the shout rose of "Death to the sea-wolves!"

Sigurd, with Biorn and another man, was far ahead of the rest, running at top speed. As the sudden attack was made, a number of Saxons sprang out from ambush and surrounded the three.

CHAPTER XI

AT ETHELRED'S COURT

SIGURD FLUNG his hand up and sheathed his sword. The Saxons paused, and one of their number stepped forward.

"You will get little plunder here, vikings, and many hard knocks," he called, "so you had best put to sea again."

"We are no vikings or sea-wolves," answered Sigurd. "I am Jarl Sigurd Buisson, one of King Olaf's men from Dublin, and am in pursuit of these men who fled up to the town. Two days since they abducted a noble lady from Olaf's own castle, whom I seek to rescue."

The Saxon leader gave an exclamation of astonishment, and at this moment Sigurd's men ran up and joined him. The Saxon bows were raised, but the leader checked them.

"You look over-young to be a Jarl," he declared, "but if your story is true we have indeed done ill. The leader of those men said he was pursued by sea-robbers, and that he was on his way to King Ethelred; so, although he was a Northman, we gave him safe conduct. What proof have you of your tale?"

Sigurd, who was in despair at this unexpected check, knew that it was necessary to win the Saxon over. "Does my ship look like a viking dragon?" he said calmly. "Were we vikings, we would not be abroad this time of year. See, I wear the Cross, and my men are from Olaf's courtmen, as you may see from their shields and weapons. We are Christians all, and no followers of Thor."

At this the Saxon stepped up and shook his hand heartily. "Your pardon, Jarl, but I am warden of the coast, and must do my utmost to defend it from sea-rovers. I am Jarl Edmund, and now I recall that in the other party was a woman, or rather girl."

"She is a noble lady of Denmark," said Sigurd, not thinking it wise to tell Astrid's real position. "Now, cannot we follow these men to the town?"

Jarl Edmund turned. "Of course, but they told us they were on the King's business, and I sent a man with them to get them horses at once. I am indeed sorry for this, Jarl."

"You but did your duty," replied Sigurd, "and there is no help for it." He looked at Biorn: "What is your counsel, old friend?"

"Ketil will push forward to London," replied Biorn, "so I think you had best follow him with the Jomsborg men, and try to catch him. I will take the others and the 'Crane,' and proceed by sea to London."

"As for you, Ketil, take heed to yourself!"

"Good!" Sigurd turned to Edmund again. "I suppose we can procure horses in the town yonder?"

"Yes," replied the Saxon, eager to repair his mistake, "I will myself go with you." Sigurd picked out his old Jomsborg men, and saying farewell to Biorn, made all haste to reach the town. As they entered, Edmund dispatched several men, one of whom returned with the news that Ketil's party had left ten minutes before. At this Edmund made a gesture of dismay.

"I fear you will not come up with them, Jarl Sigurd, for they took the best horses to be found. However, we will see what we can do."

In half an hour Sigurd and his men were riding east, Edmund having furnished them with a guide. They pushed on for many days, but found that Ketil kept well ahead, commandeering the best horses as he went, on the plea of the King's business. At Malmesbury and Wantage, Sigurd and his men were surprised at the size of the cities and the splendid civilization they found there, which was far ahead of any that the north could boast of. Wessex and Sussex had not been ravaged by the Danes for many years, and the country amazed them by its beauty and fertility.

"If these Saxons had kings like ours," remarked Sigurd to his men, "King Svein would have a hard time indeed before he could take the throne of England."

At Reading they found that Ketil was only half a day ahead of them so they pushed on to London with all speed, reaching it in the evening. Next morning Sigurd took his way to the palace.

Here he gave his name and title to the chamberlain, and was shown into the great hall, around which ran a buzz of astonishment as he appeared. Sigurd had filled out amazingly in the last few months, and was large for his age; he wore his golden helm, a blue cloth kirtle and waist, and the great sword that Olaf had given him, its hilt wound with gold and the scabbard thick with carved ivory. As he walked up the hall, he removed his helm and let his long golden hair stream over his shoulders.

The chamberlain led him to the high-seat, and Sigurd knelt a moment before King Ethelred, then rose. The king was a pale, crafty-looking man, and as Sigurd looked around his heart sank for an instant, for among the courtiers he beheld the mocking face of Ketil.

After the chamberlain announced his name and title, the King arose. "Greeting, Jarl Sigurd! The men of King Olaf are ever welcome at our court, and we look forward to another visit from himself. Well I remember Olaf, who spent a year or two with us, and I would fain see him again. You look young to hold a Jarlship under so great a man!"

Sigurd answered fittingly, then said, "My lord King, I ask your aid. Among your men I see a certain Norseman, Ketil Gormson, who not long since abducted a lady from the castle of King Olaf. I have followed him closely, and since he is here, the Lady Astrid is not far away."

King Ethelred looked surprised. "Why, what is this? The man Ketil is a peaceful trader, and arrived here only yesterday. He has told me nothing of any lady!"

"Nevertheless," replied Sigurd firmly, "she is with him, and King Olaf sent me to rescue her. I must crave your help, King Ethelred."

The king ordered Ketil to stand forth, which he did, a sly smile upon his face. Ethelred asked him what he knew of Sigurd's tale.

"Nothing, my lord; I have no woman with me, and have but just arrived by slow stages from the west coast where I was trading."

Ethelred looked at Sigurd, and then the latter knew that he was being made a mock of. No doubt the king had Astrid hid away, intending to hold her for a hostage.

"You see, Jarl Sigurd," said the king softly, "you must have been mistaken in this man, who is a kind-hearted fellow indeed. Anything that I can do to aid you will be done at once. Bring your men to the palace, and you shall be given quarters here."

At these words, and Ketil's mocking smile, Sigurd lost his temper. Taking a step forward, he cried angrily: "There is no mistake, King Ethelred, and well you know it! Think not that you will escape the heavy hand of Olaf by smooth words, when he hears of this. As for you, Ketil," Sigurd turned on the man, who shrank back at his blazing eyes, "take heed to yourself! If

I meet you outside the palace I will slay you like the dog you are!"

"You forget yourself, Jarl Sigurd," spoke out the king, sternly. "I have promised you assistance in this matter, so bring your men to the palace at once, and we will have search made for the lady."

Sigurd rejoined his men with dismay in his heart. He knew only too well that the King's command meant that he would be watched closely, and he saw no way of rescuing Astrid. When he told the men the result of his visit to court, they were as angry as he; but there was no help for it, and in the afternoon they took up their quarters in the palace.

Ketil took good care to keep out of Sigurd's way. The Jomsvikings wandered freely about the city, staring wonderingly in the shops, and Sigurd bade them keep a sharp lookout for Astrid. The days passed away, and Ethelred tried to soothe his visitors by a pretended search of the city, and by soft words, but at last Sigurd determined to take matters into his own hands. It was now the middle of February, and Sigurd was impatient to return to King Olaf.

Calling his men together after the evening meal, he said, "Men, if we are to find Lady Astrid we must do it ourselves. I believe she is held here in the palace, in the woman's wing; do you therefore hang about that side, pretending to look in the shops. I myself will do the same, and mayhap the Lady Astrid will either see us, or we will light on some clue."

Sigurd was treated with great honor, but when he went abroad he knew that he was spied upon closely. The next day he visited the shops near the women's quarters of the palace, and as he sauntered along one of his men strolled up.

"Come with me, Jarl," he whispered. Sigurd accompanied him, talking and laughing, and the man said, "Look at the third window from the end."

Sigurd did so, and his heart gave a leap of joy. There, hanging from a corner of the window, was a scrap of blue and gold cloth that he knew had been taken from Astrid's scarf. As he looked up, a face appeared, but at a quick sign of warning from him, it vanished.

"Hurrah!" he cried, when he had regained his room, "we have found her, sure enough! And now to rescue her."

That same evening he heard a wild shout go up from his men, in the next room, and a moment later Biorn strode into his room. Sigurd greeted him with unbounded joy, then seeing Biorn's face half covered with bandages, cried:

"What is this? Wounded, Biorn?"

The old viking smiled. "We met a Danish ship four days ago, Jarl, and she stopped to talk with us."

"Up to your old tricks, sea-wolf!" laughed Sigurd. "What did you talk about?"

"The price of swords, mainly," answered Skarde. "The Danes finally decided that ours were better, so we gave them Ketil's old trading ship and brought in the Dane with us; she is brand new, and as fast as the 'Crane.' It was hard work, though, for I had only thirty men, and they were double that. We lost ten killed, and half of us are wounded; but that is no matter. Now for your story."

Sigurd quickly outlined the position of himself and Astrid. When he concluded, Biorn was silent for some time.

"It is no light matter, Sigurd, to brave Ethelred; but I think we had best carry off the Lady Astrid. Once aboard the 'Crane,' we would be safe. But how to do the business?"

"By craft only, Biorn. Astrid saw me to-day, and knows we are here. How to get a message to her?"

"That is easy enough. Do you write it, and I will shoot an arrow into her window to-night."

"Good! I never thought of that." Sigurd procured a bit of parchment, and in a few minutes the message was ready. "I told her that to-morrow night we would wait beneath her window. She must contrive to let herself down, and if necessary we will fight our way down to the 'Crane.' Is she below the bridge or above it?"

"Below. I will go down to-morrow and bid the men be ready to receive us. We must get some fresh water on board, too."

An hour later Biorn returned. "The arrow flew straight, Jarl. I waited a few minutes and saw a light cross her shutter thrice."

Sigurd nodded. "Then she understands. Get the 'Crane' ready to-morrow, and return by nightfall. Better have a boat or two at the water-stairs, just at the end of this street."

"Trust me, Jarl," said the old viking, and returned to the ship.

CHAPTER XII

THE FLIGHT FROM LONDON

THE RETURN of Biorn and the finding of Astrid happened so close together that Sigurd determined to take advantage of his opportunity. He saw the King twice a day, at meals, and on each occasion Ethelred seated him near the high-seat and conversed affably with him; but Sigurd felt that the iron hand was but concealed within a silken glove, and that the King would soon find means to rid himself of this troublesome Northman.

The day after Biorn's arrival, at the noonday meal, Ethelred called Sigurd to his side as usual.

"How is the search progressing, Jarl? Have you any news yet?"

Sigurd assumed a gloomy air. "I only wish I had some, King Ethelred. My ship arrived last night, and I cannot long delay my return to King Olaf, I fear."

The King seemed unmistakably relieved, and Sigurd judged that his visit to the shops the day before had not escaped the spies. Ketil he had not seen since that first day, but as he always saw some of his men whenever he left the palace, he believed the Norseman was keeping close watch on him.

That evening Biorn entered his room shortly after dark with a coil of thin but strong rope and a light grapnel.

"Is the 'Crane' in shape?" asked Sigurd eagerly. "We had best wait an hour or two to let the streets get deserted."

"Yes, all is ready, and two large boats are waiting at the stairs. We are only three streets from the river, so the escape is open."

"I'm not so sure about that," replied Sigurd uneasily. "If Ketil discovers those boats there, and has been following you, as is likely, we may have trouble yet. However, time enough for that when it comes."

An hour later there were few people in the streets, so Sigurd roused his men and set out.

"We had better not keep together," he said. "Three of you, with Biorn, come with me; the others wait at the corner here. We will not be long."

So the four quickly made their way to the corner of the palace where Astrid's window was located. A high wall enclosed the palace, with a strip of garden inside; the palace itself had but two stories, Astrid being on the upper.

As they reached the wall, Biorn flung up the grapnel, which held, and Sigurd went up the rope, hand over hand. Changing the rope to the inside, he slid down, and stood beneath the window.

All was dark above, but when he threw up a stone at the shutter, it opened and something tumbled out. Catching it, Sigurd saw it was a rope made of shreds of curtains; he held it firm, and a minute later Astrid slid down and stood by his side.

Sigurd greeted her with a silent handclasp, and led her to the wall. Climbing up, he drew Astrid to the top, and next minute both stood in the street. Old Biorn greeted Astrid heartily, and threw a dark cloak over her dress; and without delay they started for the river.

When they met the dozen men left by Sigurd, he sent them forward with Biorn to get the boats ready, following with Astrid. Ten minutes later they descended the stairs and pushed off, Astrid and Sigurd standing in the prow of the first boat.

"Hurrah! You are free at last, Astrid!" cried Sigurd, in a low tone. At the same instant the girl pulled him sharply backward, and a spear whizzed under his arm. A yell arose, and a dark mass in front of them resolved itself into a large boat full of men.

Sigurd threw all concealment aside. "Pull, men, pull!" he shouted. One of the men sank back with a spear through him, and with that the other boat crashed into Sigurd's.

Standing in the prow, Sigurd cut with his sword at the foremost man, while Biorn endeavored to ward off the other craft. Then Ketil's mocking laugh sounded in Sigurd's ears, and as his blow fell harmlessly on the other's shield, a boat-hook caught his byrnie and all but jerked him overboard.

"You have tough bark, friend Sigurd," cried Ketil, as the boy staggered. Sigurd tried in vain to free himself from the hook, as Ketil pulled, so he cried:

"Take Astrid on board and set sail, Biorn!"

Instead of resisting the boat-hook, Sigurd gave a leap forward into the prow of Ketil's boat. As he did so, Biorn pulled away, with a cry of dismay from Astrid, and left Sigurd amid his foes.

When the boy sprang on board, Ketil was pushed back, and he staggered. Sigurd cut him down with a single blow, disengaged the hook from his steel shirt, and looked around. He had forgotten the second boat, and this was right alongside. Striking down a second man, Sigurd leaped back among his own followers.

"To the 'Crane,' men! Follow Biorn!"

The men needed no urging, and they soon caught up with the first boat. Looking back, Sigurd saw that they were not pursued, for the others were demoralized at the loss of their leader.

"All safe, Sigurd?" cried Biorn, as they came up.

"All safe," the boy replied, "and I think I have paid Ketil for his villainy. At any rate he won't bother us for some time. Row fast, men, there is no use trying to hide now."

Shouts rose on the air behind them, and they saw torches darting to and fro. Soon they passed below London Bridge, and in a few minutes were aboard the "Crane," the men on board sending up a hearty cheer.

Sigurd led Astrid to the cabin, while Biorn took charge of the ship, whose oars were already out. "Now, Astrid, tell me your story," said Sigurd, as they sat down.

"Well, about midnight that night, Ketil came to my room with a note in Runic saying that you were wounded and to come at once. I thought it strange that you should send him, but went willingly enough.

"As soon as we were outside the palace his men seized me and carried me on the ship. There I was freed, but locked in the cabin. I scratched a few words on a piece of wood, for I heard Ketil say they were going to England, and then heard you come up alongside. I threw the wood out of the window, and called, but Ketil ran in and threw a cloak over my head."

After that I was treated well enough. After we landed, Ketil made me promise not to escape if he left me free; and when we got to London King Ethelred was very nice to me, giving me women to wait on me, and many gifts."

"The villain!" cried Sigurd angrily, and he told Astrid all the king had said.

"I was kept in my room," continued Astrid, "but I had nothing to complain of. Then one day I saw you in the shops across the way, and you know the rest. I tore up some curtains to make a rope with, and here I am."

Sigurd laughed. "Well, shall we stay here, or go out on deck?"

"Out on deck, by all means. But why do your men call you Jarl?"

Sigurd told her of his last interview with Olaf, and Astrid said, casting down her eyes: "Well, I suppose after this you will hold me so far below you that—"

"Nonsense," broke in Sigurd, laughing, "get on deck and stop this foolery!"

Astrid gayly ran out on deck, and Sigurd followed. They were speeding swiftly down the Thames, which is seldom frozen in winter, and all sound of pursuit was lost. As there was nothing to be seen in the faint starlight, Astrid went to bed, Sigurd giving the cabin up to her, while he took charge of the ship, Biorn relieving him after a few hours.

At sunrise they were well at sea, and as there were plenty of furs on board, the men were warmly clad. Suddenly Sigurd, looking back, cried out:

"Look there, Biorn! What ship is that?" The old viking gave a grim laugh, and then Sigurd recollected the ship which Biorn had taken on his way to London.

"She had only fifteen men in her, Jarl, for I could spare no more from the 'Crane'; but yesterday I picked up a score of Norsemen in London, and as they were willing to take service with Olaf, they are now on board. She may come in handy."

"Yes, indeed," agreed Sigurd, "and she is a handsome ship, too. Where did you get the men, Biorn?"

"Oh!" replied the other, carelessly, "they were prisoners of Ethelred's, so I invited them to take a cruise. They were not closely watched, so there they are!"

"What have you done!" broke out Sigurd, in dismay. "Don't you know that this will bring all the Saxon forces down on us?"

Biorn shrugged his shoulders. "There were only two of Ethelred's longships lying in the water, Jarl, and seeing that they lay unwatched, some, of the men rowed over last night and all but hewed away their masts."

Sigurd seized the old viking's hand. "Pardon, Biorn, I might have known you better. That explains why we were not followed; now what shall we do?"

"Well, it is madness to put to sea in this weather, but there is no help for it. I would suggest that we either go north to Mercia or Northumberland and winter there, or else strike over to Flanders and go overland to Denmark. We would be safe enough in the north of England, for there are many vikings there and Ethelred's power is weak, to say the least."

"Then let us head for there, gather a few more men if possible, and strike for Denmark or else Flanders."

This was decided on finally, for Sigurd wished to take the captured ship with him, but his men were too few to manage both vessels in case of danger. So they coasted along the shore of East Anglia, then turned north, past the Wash, and came to the Humber River. They met with no storms on the way, though the weather was cold enough.

Just before reaching the Humber, the "Crane" stopped at a small river for fresh water. There were no habitations in sight, so Sigurd and Astrid went ashore while the casks were being filled.

"It is good to be on land again, Sigurd!" cried Astrid, after racing and beating him to the top of a small hill.

"I've been at sea so long that I don't notice it much," laughed Sigurd spreading his fur cloak in the snow for Astrid to sit on.

As they rested, looking over the broad expanse of snow, dotted with trees and forests that spread inland, they heard the ringing call of a war-horn from the ships.

"Come on, Astrid!" cried Sigurd, starting up, "something must be wrong at the ships!"

CHAPTER XIII

ALFRED OF MERCIA

THEY DASHED down the hill, and in a few minutes were through the trees and on the river bank. They found Biorn drawing up his men.

"Why, what's the matter, Biorn?"

"I am not sure, Jarl, but look up the ice yonder."

He pointed up the frozen bed of the little river, and Sigurd saw a large party of armed men, pulling a sledge, running toward them. Sigurd examined them for a minute.

"I don't think they mean to attack us, Biorn, or they would not have that sledge. They look like Saxons, so best be ready."

By this time more men had arrived from the ships, and as the Saxons approached, Sigurd saw that there were some fifty men in the party. Finding the Northmen waiting, they stopped running, and one, better dressed than the rest, in a bearskin mantle and helmet, hastened on.

As he came near, Astrid said, "Why, Sigurd, he isn't any older than you are! And you were afraid of him!"

Sigurd made no reply save a smile, for, indeed, the Saxon was only a youth, but a noble-looking one. Nearly as tall as Sigurd, he was not so broad, but his face was frank, and attracted the young Jarl at once.

"Are you Danes or Norsemen?" called the stranger.

"Norsemen," answered Sigurd, "and you are Saxons, I take it."

"Right you are," laughed the boy, with a glance over his shoulder. "Are you plundering the country?"

"Nay," answered Sigurd. "We are Christians. Bid your men stand back, for our arrows lie loosely on the strings."

The boy laughed again, as if it were a good joke, and turning, waved to his men, who halted.

"Let me explain," he said. "I am Alfred, son of Jarl Alfric of Mercia, and with me is Sigrid my sister. Briefly, we are flying from the men of King Ethelred; will you assist us?"

Sigurd, suspecting a trap, looked keenly at the boy; but his gaze was met squarely, and Sigurd's suspicions vanished. "Where is your sister, and your pursuers?" he asked.

Alfred pointed to the sledge. "My sister is ill, and we have to carry her." His face suddenly became serious. "Hasten your reply, sir Norseman, for God's sake! The King's men are not half a mile behind, and there are nigh three score of them, while half of mine are wounded or sick."

Sigurd stepped out and gripped his hand. "No time for talking, then! Take your sister and the sick or wounded men out to my ships, and let all your fighting men join mine. Take charge of him, Astrid, and use the boats quickly."

The boy called up his men, dividing them as Sigurd had ordered, and joining the Norsemen with twenty Saxons.

"We will give Ethelred's men a sharp lesson, Biorn. Do you post the men as you see fit."

A hundred yards up the river was a bend, and running toward this, Biorn motioned the men to hide behind the dry bushes that stood along the banks, while he ran forward to reconnoiter. A minute later he returned at full speed.

"Here they are," he cried. "Pass the word to wait till they come opposite, then loose arrows and at them with axes."

Barely had Biorn sunk out of sight when the pursuing party appeared, three-score Saxons under two leaders. "Pick off the leaders, men," whispered Sigurd, and as the party came between the two bands of Norsemen, Biorn's horn sounded, and a cloud of arrows poured into the compact body of Saxons. At the same time the vikings seized their swords and axes and ran forward.

The Saxons resisted bravely, but their leaders had fallen at the first fire, and after a minute of sharp hand-to-hand fighting they broke and fled.

Sigurd had headed his men, engaging a tall Saxon in single combat. The other wounded Sigurd badly in the shoulder at the first exchange of blows; and, dropping his shield, Sigurd grasped his great sword in both hands and rushed his foe. At the first blow the other's shield-arm fell, numb with the shock; at the second his sword flew from his hand and he slipped on the ice, falling heavily.

Seeing that the enemy had broken, Sigurd paused and shouted:

"Back, men, back! We only want to give them a lesson, not to slaughter them!" His own men obeyed, but Alfred's Saxons drove on after the fugitives, and Sigurd could hardly blame them. Then he turned to his foe; the man lay looking up, awaiting the death stroke.

"Get up," exclaimed Sigurd with a laugh, "I am no murderer!"

With an amazed expression, the Saxon slowly got up, and then, seizing Sigurd's hand in his, knelt and kissed it. "Thanks, lord," he said, "you are the first who ever bested Wulf at the sword, and if you will take him, he will serve you right well!"

Sigurd smiled, but faintly; and Biorn was just in time to catch him in his arms. The wounded shoulder was streaming with blood, and he had suddenly turned faint.

While Biorn held him and the other men crowded around, Wulf tore off his woolen tunic and deftly bound up the wound, Biorn watching him suspiciously; then, taking Sigurd's feet while Biorn tenderly held his body, the two carried him back to the shore.

As they approached, Astrid ran up.

"Sigurd! Is Sigurd hurt?"

"It is nothing," replied Biorn, "only a wound in the shoulder. He'll be all right in ten minutes."

Wulf, who had wounded the boy, now surprised Biorn by his tenderness. Setting the boy with his back to an ice-hummock, he bathed his face with snow, and Sigurd opened his eyes.

"Keep quiet," growled Biorn, as he struggled to rise, "I will attend to the embarking, and you can rest for a space."

By the time the water casks were aboard Alfred and the Saxons had returned, and the Saxon boy seemed genuinely sorry for his rescuer's mishap. All then embarked, and Biorn divided the men between the two ships.

On the "Crane" he took the Jomsvikings, Olaf's courtmen, and a dozen Saxons; the Norse prisoners and thirty Saxons went on board the other ship. In an hour the sails were hoisted, and the ships bore away from the land, heading east.

Sigurd sat on the forecastle of the "Crane," Astrid and the two Saxons near him. "Now tell me your story," said Sigurd, giving his own name and Astrid's.

"Our father was the Jarl of Mercia," began Alfred, "but King Ethelred has always been jealous of his popularity, and has persecuted him unceasingly. Three weeks since a party of armed men appeared to seize our father, but he fled to a Danish ship on the coast, and she took him off. My elder brother Alfgar was taken and blinded."

Astrid and Sigurd gave a cry of horror, but Alfred smiled sadly. "You do not know of what Ethelred is capable, my friends. In his present condition Alfgar is unfit to become Jarl, thus being as good as dead in the King's opinion.

"My father had barely time to send a man to warn us at Lincoln, and we fled from home just in time to get to the fens and escape. Some fourscore men, all devoted servants of my father, fled with us. Twice Ethelred's men came upon us, and we beat them off, but wounds and sickness thinned my men, and these are all I have left. Last week Sigrid came down with fever, and we had to fly again; but this time, thanks to you, we are safe. We will never forget that we owe our lives to you, Jarl Sigurd!"

Astrid immediately took charge of the sick girl. Thanks to his temperate life, Sigurd's wound promised to heal rapidly, and the man Wulf proved invaluable. He had been educated in a monastery, and was skilled in leech-craft, and seemed devoted to the boy Jarl.

"I thought to be killed at once," he told Sigurd, who had summoned him. "You are the best swordsman, as well as the only merciful viking, whom I ever met. My life is yours, Jarl, if so you will have it." The man's words were so sincere that Sigurd accepted his offer gladly, for he was an expert swordsman as well as leech, and could both read and write, which was no small accomplishment.

A council was now held on the "Crane's" forecastle, to decide on what course they should pursue. They finally came to the conclusion that they would run south and cross to Flanders, where Alfred and Sigrid would probably find their father. As soon as this course was fixed on, Biorn took charge of the "Snake," as the other vessel was named, transferring to her that evening.

It proved well, indeed, that he did so, for during the night a gale swept down out of the northeast, and bore them helplessly before it. The Saxons on the "Snake," most of whom had never been to sea before, were of little use, and even Alfred was sick, though Sigrid escaped; but there was nothing to do save to keep the ships before the wind. It was bitterly cold, but as the Norsemen did not mind this much, and the girls were well wrapped up, no one suffered greatly.

Sigurd had no fears for the two ships, for both were new and rode the waves easily. The ships of the vikings could only sail with a fair or a side wind, and as they would be driven far past Flanders unless the gale broke up soon, the four discussed the situation that evening in the "Crane's" cabin.

"We are certainly getting all the storms we want," laughed Sigurd to Astrid, as he came in and shook off the snow. "Shall we take the chances and head around for the southern end of England?"

"No!" cried Alfred. "Cannot we make for Normandy? There are many vikings there, and it is settled by Norsemen."

Sigurd shook his head. "Not unless the wind shifts."

"I see," broke in Astrid, "that you are thinking about getting me back home. I admit that I would like to see Vendland again, but why don't you just take the simplest course, Sigurd, run before the wind, then around England and back to King Olaf?"

"It sounds easy," laughed Sigurd, "and that is what I would do if I were alone. But with you and Sigrid on board I don't like to take unnecessary risks."

Sigrid laughed as Alfred, in the throes of seasickness, seized his cloak and left the cabin. "Don't mind us, Jarl; head for Ireland by all means!"

"Well," responded Sigurd, "we'll see how things look in the morning. I'm going to turn in now and get some sleep."

CHAPTER XIV

IN BRETLAND

THE MORNING broke dark and gloomy, with no land in sight. Sigurd, concluding that they had been driven below the Thames, if not below the end of England, ordered the helmsman to steer due west, and while he was unable to communicate with the "Snake," he saw Biorn follow his example at once, and knew that he understood.

The gale had now lessened to a steady wind from the north-east, interspersed with flurries of snow, and both ships drove steadily along under half-canvas.

For two days they held this course, and then Sigurd held a shouted conference with Biorn. It seemed evident that they had been carried south of England, so the prows were turned north, and the next morning land appeared. Alfred had found his sea-legs by this time, while Sigrid was rapidly gaining strength and color from the salt sea-air, which drove the marsh fever out of her. She was a very pretty girl, indeed, with her blue eyes and long flaxen hair, and she and Astrid were firm friends from the start.

Wulf, who was now more a friend than a captive, was a great favorite with all on board, even with Alfred's Saxons. On the morning that land was sighted, he drew Sigurd aside.

"Jarl, we must have fresh water at once. Three of the casks were loosened by the storm and have run out; there is only a cask or two of ale left."

Sigurd made a wry face. "Well, that will keep us from thirst, and the men like it well enough, though I have little taste for it; but perhaps we can get water from some river along the coast here, or from the 'Snake.'"

Wulf disagreed. "All Ethelred's Jarls and Thanes will be looking for us, you may be sure, and as soon as we are sighted the housecarls will be poured down wherever we land."

Sigurd thought it over, and finally signaled the "Snake." Biorn drew alongside, but when Sigurd mentioned the shortness of water, the old viking gave a cry of dismay.

"Why, we thought to get some from you! Never mind, we are drawing into the coast, and I will make a landing and find out where we are. We cannot be very far from South Wales, and once there it will be plain sailing, for the people there are of my own race, and I have not forgotten the language of the Cymry."

So they steered toward the shore, which was high and rocky. After coasting along for two or three hours, a large bay was revealed, half frozen over, with a hamlet nestling on the cliffs above.

"They are fishing folk, most like," said Alfred, "but there is no sign of a river hereabouts. We may have to melt up some of that ice!"

Biorn's ship now drew carefully in, and broke through the thin outer edge of ice. When the "Snake" would go no farther, Biorn leaped out after testing the ice with oars, and a dozen men followed him to the shore. They found the hamlet in great consternation, dreading the forays of the pirates, but Biorn soon appeased their fears, buying a goodly quantity of fish from them, and returned to the ships.

The "Snake" drew alongside the "Crane." "No fresh water, Jarl," reported Biorn. "Everything is frozen fast, and these people melt ice for their needs. They say there is a river half a mile inland, but we dare not risk it."

"I would advise that if possible we bear around South Wales and reach up for the Northern Kingdom. It will only be a day's difference, and we won't find much help among the people on this coast. We might take in some ice-cakes, in case the ale gives out."

"How long does it take to reach North Wales?" asked Sigurd.

"We ought to get there to-morrow night, or the next day at latest," replied Biorn, and Sigurd waved assent. The ships were rowed up to the ice and a supply of this was taken on board each ship; then the sails were hoisted, half the oars put out, and at full speed they passed along the coast, for Sigurd was determined not to be caught in another tempest.

Next morning, however, the Land's End was reached, and the prows turned north. By nightfall the land was in sight ahead, and early next morning they drew close into shore.

"I know where we are," shouted Biorn to Sigurd. "Do you follow me, Jarl, and we will speedily come to an open river, unless I am greatly mistaken."

Before noon, indeed, a great shout of joy went up from the men, for there before them was a bay, with an open river flowing down. True, the channel was narrow and dangerous for ships, for the ice nearly met on either side; but the "Crane" followed the "Snake" closely, and they entered the channel. Half a mile from the mouth this widened out and turned suddenly; as the "Snake" reached the bend Sigurd heard Biorn's war-horn, and saw his men arming themselves in haste.

"To arms, men!" he shouted, "and be ready for whatever may befall!" Alfred quickly donned his armor and stood by Sigurd in the prow. As they in turn came around the bend, they saw the reason for Biorn's preparations; there before them lay two large ships, moored for the winter on shore, with a camp close by. From their appearance they were Danes, and high above, on a neighboring knoll, could be seen the roofs of a town of goodly size.

As the "Crane" came alongside the "Snake," Sigurd saw that the vikings on shore were also arming and assembling around their two ships.

"This is the town of Neath, Jarl," cried Biorn, as he leaped on board the "Crane," "and it was here that I was born. What ships these are I know not; shall we draw in and hail them?"

"That would be best," replied Sigurd. "Doubtless they are some vikings who are wintering here, but it is strange, indeed, that they are allowed to remain so near a town, unless they came on a peaceful errand."

Sigurd ordered the men to row as close to shore as they could. The ship stopped two or three hundred yards from it, for it was impossible to break through the ice, and Sigurd blew a loud blast on a peace-horn. In answer came one from the camp, and a dozen men left the two ships and started over the ice toward the "Crane." As these came near, Astrid uttered a little cry and caught Sigurd's arm. "Oh, Fairhair, look at that big man in front! That is Halfdan, the brother of Queen Gunhild, and my own uncle!"

Sigurd looked closely at the man, remembered him well, for he had seen him often while the Jomsborg men were at King

Svein's court. Halfdan stopped just beyond spear-cast of the "Crane."

"Who are you, and do you come in peace or war?" he called.

"Good-morning!" laughed Sigurd, "don't you know your friends, Jarl?"

The other started, looked keenly at the ship, and ran forward. "Surely, it is Sigurd Fairhair!" he cried, as he came near. "And by the eye of Odin! Am I dreaming or is this Astrid?"

"Astrid it is, uncle!" laughed the girl, jumping down on the ice and throwing her arms around his neck. The Jarl struggled to disengage himself, and cried in mock dismay:

"Help; help, are you trying to make me captive? Let loose! Respect my dignity!"

Sigurd followed Astrid to the ice, and clasped Halfdan's hand. "Be careful, uncle," laughed Astrid, "Sigurd is your equal in dignity now!"

Sigurd nodded at the surprised look of the Dane. "Yes, I am one of Olaf Tryggveson's men now, Jarl, and he made me a Jarl lately, although I am altogether too young for such an honor."

"Nonsense, nonsense!" replied Halfdan, his merry eyes gleaming with happiness, "you are the handsomest Jarl I ever saw in my life, upon my word! But come up to the camp."

"Wait," said Sigurd, turning to his ships. "Alfred, do you and Sigrid join us. Wulf, you and Biorn take charge of the ships and lay them up on shore, there beside the others. We are with friends."

As Alfred and Sigrid climbed down to the ice, the young Jarl presented them to Halfdan, who greeted them heartily.

"I have heard of your father's misfortune," he exclaimed, "and I was sorry, indeed, for I fought against him three or four years ago, and he was a noble foeman. However, he is safe in Flanders now, and is like to return before long."

"Why, what do you mean?" cried Alfred, in surprise.

"Come along to the camp and I'll tell you." Halfdan led the way to the shore. "It's too cold to be standing out here talking."

As they entered the camp, the news spread that a party of Jomsvikings were among the arrivals, and a loud blast went up from the horns, while the Danes met them with shouts of joy, for the men of Jomsborg were prime favorites with King Svein's men. Sigurd found several whom he knew, while Astrid was met with fresh cheers. As they entered the large hut of Halfdan, the Jarl drove the men off.

"Get out of here!" he cried. "Go down and help stow the ships up on land beside ours. We have much to talk over here, and would be left in peace."

With a last cheer, the men vanished, and Halfdan closed the door.

"Here is food and water, friends, if you are hungry."

"We have plenty of food, but a drink of water would not be amiss," answered Sigurd. "And now, how come you here, in Wales?"

"First make yourselves comfortable." Halfdan piled furs along the wall, for Astrid and Sigrid, while he and the two boys sat on the long wooden bench. "Well, of course you remember the oath that Svein made that night? He wasn't in such a hurry as you Jomsvikings were, but he has been making big preparations. He sent me here right after the news of Hiorunga Bay arrived, for he had counted on your men making a descent on Ethelred from the west as well as from Northumbria, where he himself will land in the spring or summer.

"I arrived here a month or two ago, and have arranged matters with Idwal ap Meirig, the King of North Wales. What barbarous names these Welsh people have!"

"Probably they think ours just as bad," laughed Sigrid, "for they hate everything Saxon; and as for your Norse names, I am sure they used to sound harsh, even to us!"

"Well, in any case, King Idwal is up in the town yonder, has agreed to join us, and we see him nearly every day. Now, tell me something about yourself, Sigurd."

It was late when Sigurd finished his tale, so Halfdan, who had given orders meanwhile, showed the two girls to a hut that had been hastily fitted up for them, and shared his own with the boys for the night.

CHAPTER XV

IN WINTER QUARTERS

NEXT MORNING Halfdan's men joined forces with the new arrivals, and got the two ships up on the shore, dismantling and unloading them, while parties of men hastened out to the surrounding woods, and returned with great quantities of firewood and timber, with which fresh huts were built.

This was finished by evening, for Halfdan had a hundred and fifty men, and many hands made light labor. For several days the Norsemen rested quietly, for they had many wounded, and some of the Saxons were still down with fever. Sigrid, however, was now almost well, and the jovial roughness of Halfdan amused her and brought the roses back to her cheeks.

Sigurd and Alfred wished to visit the town above, and if possible to take up their quarters there, but Halfdan discouraged them from doing so.

"King Idwal watches us sharp enough, for he has suspicions of every Northman within a hundred miles. One cannot blame him, either; the vikings have ravaged poor Bretland terribly, destroying monasteries and towns, and burning and plundering. Your own man Biorn is a sample; he was carried off in his youth.

"As for visiting the town, it is not worth while. There is nothing there save a great castle and a cluster of dirty little houses, and in any case Idwal has forbidden our men to enter the town. Once a week the country folk come down here with their market stuff, and Idwal sends us ale by the cask. Never fear, he will be down pretty soon to see for himself who these new vikings are."

For two weeks they remained in camp, seeing nothing of the Welsh king, but all were greatly interested in the people, who brought fresh meat and food into camp once a week. Indeed, the vikings' camp at these times assumed the appearance of a fair, for most of the men made small objects which the country people took in exchange, and many merchants set up permanent booths inside the camp. The Welsh people were smaller by far than the Norsemen or Danes, and their bright, quick eyes and black straight hair contrasted strangely with the Northmen and Saxons, most of whom were fair.

Sigurd and Alfred had at first feared that the Saxons and Danes, hereditary enemies, would not mingle well; but their fears proved to be unfounded. Halfdan discovered from the country people that in the forests to the west, only a few miles distant, wolves were a terrible scourge; so the men set to work and made skis for themselves, and even Sigrid learned to use the "snow-skates," as the Saxons called the long wooden runners. In the second week of their stay the four young people and Halfdan took a score of men, leaving the camp in charge of Biorn, and for three days went off on a wolf-hunt in the forest.

On their return Biorn told them that word had arrived in their absence from King Idwal, who intended to visit them on the following day, with all his court. Great preparations were made for his reception. Pine boughs were brought in from the forest, with which the huts were decorated gayly, and Halfdan's large hut was hung with tapestries and cloths, which Sigurd found in the cargo of the vessel which Biorn had captured.

All the men rubbed up their armor and weapons, and when in the morning the Welsh were seen winding down the hill, the force was drawn up in three divisions, the Danes, Norsemen and Saxons grouping themselves together under the standards of Halfdan, Sigurd and Alfred. Presently the Welsh arrived in the valley leading to the camp, and their coming was greeted by a loud burst from the horns of the vikings.

Leading the way came a troop of archers, behind whom, mounted on small shaggy ponies, rode the King and his court.

Idwal was a larger man than most of his followers, with keen black eyes and firm features, shaved in the Danish fashion, with two long mustaches. As he came up Halfdan advanced and greeted him.

"Welcome, my lord King! It gives us pleasure to return the hospitality of your castle!"

Idwal smiled. "Truly, Jarl, I am glad that these men of yours are not minded to foray my borders! We would have a hard time of it to repel such a force as this. I heard that you had been joined by a fresh band of vikings, so came down to assure myself that we were in no danger."

At this Halfdan motioned Sigurd and his friends to advance and presented them to the King. The latter frowned as Alfred came forward, and swept his eye over the band of Saxons.

"It is many years since a Saxon has dared seek hospitality from the Cymry, my lad," he remarked. Then Alfred told his story, and the king's face cleared.

"Well, to be frank, I have small love for Saxons, but since you are enemies of Ethelred, that is another matter. Tell me, in case your father returned home and I joined with King Svein, would you be for or against me?"

He gazed keenly at Alfred, but the lad met the look squarely, though with a smile. "As to that, my lord King, I can only say that I would fight for my own land against the invader, whoever he was; yet if my father thinks it right to join King Svein, as well he may, I will be at his side."

Halfdan broke in with a laugh. "Don't be afraid, my lord, this Saxon will not have to be feared for some time to come! I dare say that if you make a foray against Ethelred this spring, he would stand as stoutly at your side as any of your nobles. But come into the camp, my lord."

The vikings opened a path between their ranks, and Idwal led his men through them. In an open space amid the huts, Halfdan had cleared away the snow and stretched a large sail over a number of long tables, while on either side blazed a dozen great fires.

"By my faith," cried King Idwal, "this is a right royal reception, Jarl! An open air banquet is far more to my liking than one inside these huts, and these fires would warm an army!"

So saying, the king tossed aside his fur cloak, and Sigurd saw that he wore a light suit of armor beneath it. In the king's train were some twoscore nobles, and a bishop, to whom Halfdan accorded the place of honor. Among the Welsh, bishops and priests were honored even above the king, and they found Bishop Dafydd a learned, kindly, and intensely religious man, who was at once interested in Astrid and Wulf, with both of whom he conversed at great length.

It was well, indeed, that Halfdan had been hunting for three days previously, for his stock of venison was heavily drawn upon. Great fish were brought in, newly taken from the river below, and to the delight of the Welshmen a huge boar's head, in the Saxon style, was placed before the king. The vikings spared no pains to make the feast a notable one, and to Sigurd's satisfaction the presence of Bishop Dafydd and his men prevented it from becoming a wild carouse, as the Norsemen were only too apt to make it.

Before the King left that evening there was an exchange of gifts, as was customary. Biorn and Jarl Halfdan, who were skillful smiths, had the week before made a beautiful byrnie, of woven gold rings, and this was presented to the king, who was delighted with it.

He presented Halfdan with a great boarhound, and to Sigurd he gave a cloak, edged with fur, the scarlet cloth embroidered in silver thread. As he had been informed of the presence of the two girls, he had thoughtfully brought for them new outfits of garments suited to their rank.

Idwal returned to his castle that evening, and the bond between him and the vikings was firmly cemented. He assured Jarl Halfdan that as soon as King Svein landed in the east he

They were greeted by a load burst from the horns of the vikings.

would pour a flood of men over the West Saxon earldoms, and Halfdan had no doubt that the Danish king would fulfill the oath he had sworn at his accession feast.

After this the camp settled down for the remainder of the winter. Every week hunting parties, on skis, brought in fresh meat from the surrounding forests, while their arms were repaired and added to by the smiths. The chiefs of the Northmen were all trained armorers, and his work at the forge added greatly to Sigurd's strength and widened his shoulders immensely.

The two girls had a most enjoyable time, for every man in the camp worshiped them. They joined the hunting parties, and many a wolf fell before Astrid's bow, while Sigrid, though less warlike, took part with equal zest.

The time passed away rapidly, and in March the snows melted and the four ships were run out and overhauled. They were freshly pitched and calked, the masts were stepped, and at last they lay at anchor, fully ready for the sea.

King Idwal paid the camp a second visit, after which the chiefs returned to the castle with him for a few days. He sent down provisions of all kinds for the ships, and at the beginning of April, Sigurd took leave of Halfdan.

They gathered in the Jarl's hut on the evening before sailing.

"Now, Jarl," said Sigurd, "I suppose you will take Astrid home with you?"

"That depends," replied Halfdan, quizzically, "upon whether she wants to go or not! She seems to like wandering about the world, with a knight-errant to rescue her and guard her from harm!"

Astrid blushed, and cried, "That's not fair, uncle! I'm going home with you—but listen! Why can't you come with us to King Olaf, and go home by the north? It is just as short that way, and far less dangerous!"

The big Jarl leaped to his feet. "Hurrah! I never even thought of that; I thought to go home around the south of England, but in truth this way is as short, and I would fain see this King Olaf, whom you praise so highly."

It had been arranged that Halfdan was not to sail till the next week, so he at once dashed out and called his chiefs together. Telling them of the new plan, the men went to work, by torchlight, and finished loading his two ships, and by morning all was ready.

With a fair wind they reached out into the bay, and three mornings later, after coasting along the Irish shore, they came in sight of the towers of Dublin.

CHAPTER XVI

AN AMBUSCADE

SIGURD WAS received with unbounded joy by King Olaf, for he had been given up for lost in the storm that swept the coast just before his departure. Halfdan stayed in Dublin for a week, then decided to return home without further delay.

Sigurd parted with Astrid sorrowfully, for they had become very dear to each other in their wanderings, and although Alfred and Sigrid remained with him, he knew that he would miss her greatly.

"Never mind," he said, as they walked down to the ships, "we will land in Norway this summer or fall, and be sure that I will turn up at the Danish court, or in Vendland, not long after."

"I'll be glad to see Vagn once more, when I get home," said Astrid. "It will seem almost as good as seeing you." Halfdan had told them of Vagn's safe arrival home, so that Jarl Eirik had evidently been true to his word.

Sigurd and Alfred, in the "Crane," accompanied Halfdan's ships for a few miles; then, with a last farewell to Astrid, the "Crane" was turned about, and sought Dublin again.

Sigurd's duties were light at the court. Olaf's Irish kingdom was not divided in districts, ruled by Jarls, as was Norway; so that Sigurd had little to do beyond commanding the courtmen. Alfred had not done homage to King Olaf, for he resolved to remain true to his own land; nevertheless, the King gave him a command, and Alfred bore himself well indeed.

With the beginning of summer Olaf took all his warships out of the water, scraped the bottoms, and gave them a thorough overhauling. Thorir Klakke was still in Dublin, and Sigurd found that he was urging the King to sail as soon as might be for Norway, saying that the bonders would flock to him on his arrival, so that he need not take so large a force. King Olaf, who thoroughly understood his treachery, did not undeceive him; but to Sigurd he said, one night after Thorir had left the hall:

"Jarl, if ever a man deserved hanging, there is one. While you were absent in England, two half-brothers of mine were driven from Norway by Jarl Hakon, and came to me here. Thorir tried to bribe them, and fortunately they let him think that they fell in with his plans, which he disclosed fully.

"Jarl Hakon, in truth, sent him here. Thorir will try to slay me on the voyage," the King smiled grimly, "but if he fails, he is to get me on shore at a certain point where Hakon will keep men in waiting day and night. These men are to fall on me and kill me."

Sigurd gave a cry of anger, and the priest, Thangbrand, growled out, "Let me attend to him, Olaf! I'll warrant he does not trouble you any more!"

Olaf laughed heartily. "Thangbrand, you are more fitted for a viking than for a priest! If I ever win Norway, I will send you to Iceland to convert that island to Christ."

The priest's face lit up. "Thanks, my King! It is a shame that so fair an island as that should have no church of Christ in all its length! It may be that I will meet resistance there, but methinks I can hold my own."

Sigurd laughed at this characteristic speech. Thangbrand was a strange mixture of priest and warrior. Driven from home for his quarrelsome disposition, he had joined himself to Olaf; but in reality the man was deeply religious, and he was, indeed, the ideal man to carry the Cross to heathen Iceland. In those days the Cross and sword went together, and the old gods of Norway knew many martyrs to their faith before Christianity was established in the land, in later years. Right or wrong, this was the spirit of the age, for men overlooked the fact that Christ's gospel was one of peace, and in their enthusiasm and religious fervor they spread it with fire and sword.

There was much irregular fighting around Dublin, for the Irish kings were ever striving to drive the Norsemen from their land. They fought bravely, but their men were ill-armed compared with the vikings, and Olaf had no trouble in preserving order for many miles around the city. His brother-in-law, Olaf Kvaran, was away on a trip to Iceland at this time.

"How would you like, Jarl," said Olaf to Sigurd one evening, "to visit King Brian Boroimhe? I am minded to make peace with him, for when I go to Norway I want to leave Dublin in security, and my brother is not to be relied on. A firm peace with King Brian for at least a year would be an excellent thing."

"I would be glad, indeed," replied Sigurd, "for I have heard so much about the interior of Ireland that I would fain see it."

"Well, I will have letters written in the Irish tongue," said the King, "and do you take what men you will, together with an interpreter. Be ready to start next Monday, and I think you will find the King at Kells, a large place some thirty miles to the west. However, I will provide a reliable guide."

Thangbrand, the priest, hearing of the embassy, eagerly sought leave to accompany Sigurd, which Olaf willingly granted. So, on the following Monday, Sigurd, the priest, and a score of men left Dublin. Their weapons were all in peace-bands, and an Irish captive was taken as guide and interpreter, having promised to lead them to Kells in exchange for his liberty.

Sigurd laughed when Thangbrand joined the party. The huge priest wore a byrnie under his gown, a light steel cap on his head, and at his saddle-bow was shield and sword.

"No one knows what may happen," he replied stoutly, to the boy's peal of laughter, "we may be waylaid by these Irish thieves, or this guide may lead us astray, and it is best to be prepared for anything."

Kells was only a good day's march away, so they set forward briskly. After reaching the bounds of Olaf's territory the road lay through woods and swamps for a dozen miles; but toward evening they emerged on an open plain, partly cultivated, and saw in the distance the spires and towers of a large city. Several times they had been stopped by bands of Irish, but their guide served them faithfully.

Sigurd was amazed at sight of Kells. "Why, this is wonderful!" he said. "I had no idea that there was such civilization so near to Dublin!"

Thangbrand smiled. "Kells has seldom been ravaged by vikings, for many years; it is a strong place, with a great monastery in the town. I have been here once before, and found that the land is beautiful enough in times of peace, but in wartime it would be well-nigh impossible to reach the city."

Sigurd saw that this was so, as they approached, for on either side of the road were defenses, and several stone castles came in sight. Just at sunset they entered the gates of the town, and their guide spurred ahead to find quarters for the men.

As they passed through the streets they met with sour looks and loud curses from the Irish, who hated the Northmen bitterly, with only too much reason. The vikings had ravaged the fairest vales of Erin, had destroyed her monasteries and splendid civilization, and but for the strong hand of King Brian would have overrun the country utterly. That night they took their quarters in a large inn, and the next morning visited the court.

The King's palace was far beyond anything Sigurd had ever seen, even in London. It was built of stone, and the great hall within was a blaze of arms and tapestries. The nobles who thronged the hall were clad much as were the Northmen, but their golden bracelets and cloak-pins were richly wrought, and the precious metal seemed abundant.

Sigurd led his men to the high-seat, and bowed low to King Brian, the famous chieftain. The latter was a powerful, stern-faced man of some sixty years, and he opened and read the letters of Olaf with a frown, afterwards handing them to a monk who stood at his side.

"Sir Jarl," he said, without rising, fixing his gray eyes on Sigurd, "I will have an answer written at once. For the present you and your men will be quartered in my palace here. King Olaf is a brave and worthy man, and I am glad to conclude a year's truce with him; were other Northmen like him, Erin would be a happier land."

The monk translated the King's words, and bowing low, Sigurd retired. Thangbrand at once visited the monastery, taking Sigurd with him; and although the good monks were somewhat surprised at the warlike appearance of the priest, they entertained their visitors well, and showed them over the buildings.

Next morning Sigurd had another audience with King Brian, who handed him a parchment for King Olaf, and presented him with a heavy golden arm-ring; after which the Norsemen left the city at once on their return journey.

They rode along at a good pace, and as they came near the boundaries of Olaf's territory Sigurd and Thangbrand rode somewhat ahead of the party; for Thangbrand, who was an adept at horsemanship, of which the young Jarl knew little, was showing Sigurd how to make his steed curvet and prance, and thus they insensibly drew ahead of the rest.

They turned a bend in the road, which wound along beneath thick trees; and as they did so a number of men sprang to their horses' heads, and others sprang at Sigurd and Thangbrand, striving to pull them from their saddles. At the same instant, before they could grasp their weapons, men dropped on them from the branches overhead, and a minute later the two Norsemen, bound hand and foot, were being hurried away through the forest depths.

CHAPTER XVII

KETIL TURNS UP

FAR BEHIND them sounded a few faint shouts and horns, as the men reached the spot where the two leaders had been ambushed; then these died away into silence. Sigurd saw that they were carried by a band of two dozen Irish, who were hastening north through the forest. He started to speak to the priest, who was borne at his side, but one of the men struck him roughly on the mouth, with a sharp command in Irish, and he ceased.

At nightfall the band halted beside a stream, and Sigurd judged they had traveled several miles from the scene of their capture. A blazing fire was built, over which the men cooked their meal, the two captives being flung down beneath a large tree.

"What fools we were to leave the guide!" growled Thangbrand into his thick black beard. "I wish they would give us somewhat to eat."

His wish was gratified immediately, for the leader of the band approached, cut the ropes that bound their hands, and gave them bread and meat, and a horn of water from the stream. After this they were bound again.

"They seem to be expecting someone," exclaimed Sigurd, "did you note that the leader had sent men out in all directions?"

This had indeed been done as soon as they arrived, and an hour later there was a shout, and into the firelight came a second body of men. As they saw them, Sigurd gave a cry of amazement, for at their head was Ketil Gormson, whom he had left in London the winter before!

The new arrivals were also Irish, Ketil being the only foreigner. The leader of the first party greeted him, and Ketil put into his hand a bag that clinked pleasantly. Then he stepped forward to Sigurd's side.

"So I have you at last, my lord Jarl!" he cried, an evil light in his dark eyes. "It is a far cry from London to Ireland, but I have watched and waited patiently."

"It is a pity that I didn't strike harder that night!" replied Sigurd. "What is your object in this attack?"

Ketil laughed shortly. "You go with me to Jarl Hakon, my fine fellow, and as for this follower of the white Christ, I think I will turn him over to these good friends of mine in the morning."

Sigurd turned pale, for he knew that any Norsemen who fell into the hands of the Irish obtained short shrift. Thangbrand, however, roared out:

"Loose my hands, you traitor, and face me with drawn blade!"

"So," sneered Ketil, "I thought that priests of your God were meek and humble men, willing to die for their faith!"

Thangbrand flushed under the reproof, and fell silent. Ketil turned away, set a guard over the captives, and in a few minutes the band lay sleeping in their cloaks beneath the trees.

The Norsemen's weapons had not been taken from them, but as they were bound firmly they were of no use. Sigurd, however, saw that the peace-bands had been torn from his sword in the hasty flight through the forest.

An hour after this he felt Thangbrand's hands touch his. The two captives lay side by side, and their guard was sitting a few feet away, nodding sleepily. Turning by inches, Sigurd looked at the priest, and saw him motion toward the unbound sword.

Sigurd, very slowly and cautiously, rolled over on his face, bringing the weapon within reach of Thangbrand, who at the same time turned his back. Thus his hands, after a little vain searching, met the hilt of the weapon and slowly drew it forth. An instant later their guard straightened up and strolled over to them. Sigurd lay on his face, and with a quick movement Thangbrand had thrust the drawn blade beneath him. The guard, thinking that both were asleep, turned away, humming an air, and Sigurd caught a faint rasping noise as the sword blade cut through the priest's bonds.

Soon the guard returned, and stooped over Sigurd, who lay nearer him, to assure himself that his bonds were right. As he did so, Thangbrand drew him down to the earth, his hands about the man's throat.

The struggle was brief and noiseless. In a few seconds the man relaxed, and the priest quickly bound and gagged him; then he cut Sigurd's bonds, whispering:

"If my hands were not so stiff I would have done better."

Indeed, Sigurd found that his hands and feet were too stiff to move, for he had been tightly bound. They both sat for a moment rubbing their limbs, then arose.

"Which way, Jarl?"

"West, Thangbrand. Once we strike men belonging to King Brian we will be all right, for his bracelet here will be known, and you are a priest, too."

Without a word more they stepped away, each picking up a light shield from beside the sleeping men as they went. The forest was dark, but as the moon was just rising Sigurd knew that their way would soon be light enough to travel fast.

In half an hour they were well away from the camp, and both broke into a swift trot, threading their way among the trees, and as far as they were able heading west. The trees were roughly barked on the north, and this guided them somewhat, for both men were accustomed, at home in Norway, to finding their way through the forest by such signs.

"Hold up, lad," panted Thangbrand, after an hour's running.

Sigurd slackened his pace, for the ground was too uneven and rough to keep it up longer, and for a time they walked swiftly onward.

"Pray heaven that we strike no bog or morass," said Thangbrand, "for if we do we are lost."

"I wonder if we will be pursued?"

"If we are, I do not propose to fall into their hands alive," answered the priest, stoutly. "They are evidently some wandering band, who have been hired by that villain Ketil. I'd like to get him within reach of my sword!"

They kept onward till dawn, walking and running by turns. As the gray light broke through the trees, they found that the forest was thinning out somewhat, and Thangbrand flung himself down for a brief rest.

"I think we must be getting near the cultivated fields in that broad plain we crossed yesterday," conjectured Sigurd. "If we can once get to Brian he will protect us, for I have heard that no one could be more jealous of his word than he."

Ten minutes later they continued their way. The sun was just rising now, and as they stood on the top of a small hill, vainly endeavoring to see some signs of habitation, a faint yell arose from the forest behind them.

"Come on, Thangbrand," exclaimed Sigurd, breaking into a run. "It is a matter of speed now."

For half an hour they kept up a brisk trot, but could hear the yells rising from time to time behind them, each louder than the last. Finally Thangbrand stopped short.

"Go on, Fairhair. I am clean winded, and your life is worth more than mine to Olaf. Do you go on, while I hold them here as long as may be."

"One of the Jomsborg oaths," replied Sigurd, quietly, "is to never desert a comrade—"

"Out upon your Jomsborg oaths!" roared Thangbrand. "Get you gone, and lose no time!"

"Listen!" cried Sigurd quickly. "Isn't that a horn?"

Far off toward the west they heard the faint notes of a war-horn, while from behind them a loud shout arose, as their pursuers came in sight.

"Hasten, Fairhair," cried the priest, unsheathing his sword. "Go yonder and bring help while I hold them here!"

Sigurd smiled and unsheathed his own weapon, as he looked around.

"Cease this nonsense," he said, though not without a thrill at thought of the generosity of the big man. "Let us stand beneath this big oak, where we can swing our swords without being struck in the back."

They took position on either side of a large oak tree, and five minutes later the first of their pursuers appeared. He halted at seeing them, and sent up a yell; as his comrades came up, they spread out, enclosing the tree in a circle.

To do him justice, Ketil was brave enough. When he appeared, he led a dozen men straight at the tree, and in a second the two were fighting furiously. The Irish crowded around, striking with their long knives, but speedily recoiled before the terrible sweep of Thangbrand's huge sword, and the more scientific, but no less deadly, blows of the young Jarl. As they retired, their chief yelled an order, and the arrows began to whizz past.

The first Sigurd caught with his shield, the second he cut in two as it flew. A shout of amazement went up from the Irish as Thangbrand did the same, for, unacquainted as they were with the exercises and training of the Norsemen, this skill seemed little less than magical. Again and again the two men repeated the trick, but it was impossible to ward off more than one or two shafts at a time, and soon both Thangbrand and Sigurd were wounded. Suddenly Ketil sprang at Sigurd with a shout of impatience.

The Irish circled around, watching the combat with eager eyes, forgetful of all else, while Thangbrand guarded Sigurd's back. Thrice Ketil's steel met that of Sigurd, then seeing an opening, the latter struck; but his feet slipped on the dew-wet grass, and he fell headfirst.

Thangbrand was instantly bestriding his body, facing Ketil. At this the Irish came in behind him, watching eagerly for a chance to use their long knives, while the priest crossed swords with Ketil. Suddenly the latter threw up his arms as something flew past Thangbrand, and fell with a spear through his body as a yell of terror went up from his band.

Looking about as he raised Sigurd to his feet, Thangbrand saw King Brian Boroimhe behind him, sword in hand, while his men pursued the fleeing band in all directions, cutting them down without mercy.

CHAPTER XVIII

A MISSION FOR THE KING

THE KING addressed Thangbrand in Latin, which the priest understood fairly well.

"Just in time, my friends! The guide whom I sent with you returned late last night with word of your mishap, and early this morning I sent men in all directions, joining myself in the search, for I was greatly angered that my safe-conduct had been broken in this wise."

"We owe you our lives, my lord," responded Thangbrand gratefully. "These men were in the pay of a traitor, whom your spear slew before I had a chance at him, unfortunately."

The old king smiled, not unkindly. "Strange words for a man of God, sir priest! But I see that your blade has done good service to Jarl Sigurd, and perhaps in these times a priest must be man of the world as well." King Brian sighed heavily as he looked around, then said, "Ask the Jarl if he has my letters safe."

When Thangbrand translated, Sigurd held up the letters, their seals unbroken; and now the King's men returned, and the party went to Kells at once. Here, as Sigurd was in haste to get back to Dublin, the King gave him an escort of fifty men, and they set out without delay.

Upon reaching the territory of Olaf, Sigurd dismissed the Irish and pushed forward; but on coming within sight of the city he gave an exclamation of dismay. Instead of the King's standard, there floated from the castle a huge black banner!

Wondering greatly, they galloped up to the city and entered. To their amazement, the shops were all closed, and the whole city wore an air of mourning. Sigurd, without stopping to ask questions, left Thangbrand and hurried to the great hall.

It was empty, save for Olaf, who sat in the high-seat, his head bowed in his hands. Sigurd advanced and held out the letters.

"Here, my lord, is the reply of King Brian Boroimhe. Why is the black standard on the castle, and why are all the shops shut?"

Olaf raised his head and gazed at Sigurd with heavy eyes.

"Welcome back, Jarl, in an evil hour. Queen Gyda died last night."

As Sigurd stared at the King, the latter rose slowly, descended from the high-seat, and taking Sigurd's arm in his, exclaimed: "Sigurd, come and talk to me. I am lonely, and the most wretched of all men."

They walked up and down the hall, and Olaf told Sigurd how the night before the Queen had been seized with a fatal illness. Good Bishop Sigurd, the English prelate who had come to Ireland with Olaf, had done his best, for he was a skillful leech, but to no avail.

"Why should this evil come upon me now?" cried the King, bitterly. Sigurd said little, allowing the King's pent-up grief to find utterance, then he said, softly:

"It is the will of God, Olaf, and perhaps he has done it for the best. May it not be that he means you to give your whole life to the spreading of his Word in heathen Norway, and has sent you a touch of adversity to try you?"

"Mayhap," responded the King, "but it is hard. He has given me good fortune, and I must bear the bad when it is his will; it may be true that he wishes me to devote myself, heart and soul, to bearing his gospel to my countrymen."

The blow was a terrible one to Olaf, and it was indeed many a month ere he recovered a portion of his former lighthearted spirits. Two days later the Queen was buried, and after the period of mourning Olaf threw himself into the work of preparing the expedition with feverish energy.

This was no light task, indeed. Olaf had a dozen warships in the harbor, but it was impossible to take so large a force, as men had to be left to defend Dublin. Olaf had decided to give up his Irish land, in case of succeeding in Norway, to his brother-in-law, Olaf Kvaran, but he could not leave him without men.

At last, after many consultations with Sigurd and his other chiefs, the King decided to take only the five largest ships, which would hold about seventy-five men each. Thorir Klakke had no inkling that Olaf knew of his treachery, and he advised the King to make a sudden descent on Norway and to take Jarl Hakon unawares at Thrandheim, before men could be gathered. Thorir, in giving this advice, thought that either he would be able to kill Olaf by treachery on the voyage, or else that the men of Hakon, posted at Agdaness in Norway, would remove Olaf before the plan could be accomplished.

The five ships were fitted up in the best of shape. The dragon heads were taken from their prows, and in the place of these great crosses were set up, for Olaf knew that only by the favor of God would he be able to win his father's kingdom. They were laden with all the wealth that Olaf had gathered in his travels through Russia, Constantinople, and England, and at length the expedition was ready to start.

It was a bright morning in August that the King went on board his ships, followed by all his men. Before doing so, he called Alfred and Sigrid to him, and asked them what they intended to do. Alfred hesitated, for although he wished to accompany Olaf, he did not forget that his father was in Flanders, and he did not like to separate from his sister. Finally, Olaf said, with a smile:

"You both had best come with me. I have a plan which I think will work out to your satisfaction; I will tell you later just what it is. Put all your Saxons on board the 'Snake,' Alfred—the ship that old Biorn captured in England, and sail with us. Sigurd will command the 'Crane,' and when we get to the Orkneys I will tell you what I have in mind."

So, wondering what the King meant, the "Snake" was added to the fleet, to Sigurd's great joy. He had feared that Alfred and his sister would be left behind, and it was with no small satisfaction that he helped fit out the "Snake."

When the men were all embarked, Bishop Sigurd, standing in the prow of King Olaf's ship, offered up a solemn prayer asking the aid and the blessing of God for their enterprise. As he concluded, a great "Amen!" rolled over the sea from ships to shore, the anchors were weighed, and the journey was begun amid a blare of war-horns and the clash of arms.

The Pentland Firth was not passable, according to reports brought to Olaf, so he bore up for the Orkneys, as had been his wish from the first. These islands had long been settled by Norsemen, and Jarl Sigurd Lodvarson ruled them; but the Jarl and his people were all heathen, for no missionaries or Christian men had been allowed to settle in the islands. It was Olaf's firm intention to spread the Word of God wherever he went, and as the Orkneys were in his path, he decided to visit Jarl Sigurd.

This was a dangerous proceeding, for the Jarl was powerful, and might have settled the fate of the expedition there and then; but matters came out luckily for Olaf. His six ships came to anchor in Asmundar Bay, in Rognwald Island, and in the bay they found a single ship lying at anchor.

Olaf, seeing that the ship was a fine one, and very beautifully furnished, dispatched Sigurd Fairhair to bring her commander on board his own ship, hoping to get news of Norway. To his surprise, it happened that this commander was no other than Jarl Sigurd Lodvarson himself!

Olaf greeted him with a smile. "Truly, it seems that we have an abundance of Sigurds here! Yourself, my own Jarl Sigurd Fairhair, good Bishop Sigurd, of England, and possibly a score of my men, all named alike."

The Jarl, not knowing where King Olaf was bound with his fleet, was somewhat fearful for his safety, and when Olaf urged him to be baptized, he refused, saying the faith of his fathers was good enough for him. Then King Olaf arose, holding in one hand a sword, in the other a cross.

"Jarl, you hold, as Jarl of the Orkneys, part of my inheritance, for I claim all the lands as mine which the Kings of Norway have possessed. As it has come to pass, by the will of God, that you are in my power, there are two courses open to you. The one, that you accept the true faith, and allow yourself to be baptized, with all your subjects. You may expect to hold under me the Jarldom which you now possess, and what is of more importance, you may hope to reign for ever in a nobler kingdom than this.

"The other course, a very wretched one, is that you die; and after your death I will pass over the islands and bring the folk to believe in the true God. Now choose, Jarl, which course you will take."

The Jarl hesitated; then he slowly stretched out his hand and took the cross from that of Olaf. This action was greeted with glad shouts from the crews, and without delay Bishop Sigurd baptized Jarl Sigurd.

Then he swore oaths of fidelity to King Olaf, and placed in the King's hands his son, Hundi, who was also baptized, and who accompanied Olaf to Norway as a hostage.

Next day Olaf came on board the "Crane."

"Sigurd," he said, "are you willing to undertake another mission for me? You seem to scrape through somehow, no matter what happens, and as this one is of some importance I can think of no one better fitted to undertake it."

Sigurd smiled. "If I have scraped through some tight places, Olaf, I don't ascribe it to my own conduct! I have been fortunate in finding friends, and for the rest, God has protected me. Now tell me what this mission is."

CHAPTER XIX

AT KING SVEIN'S COURT

ASTRID AND Halfdan had a safe and quiet voyage home to Denmark, but when they arrived there they found that many changes had taken place during the winter. The pale, quiet, religious Queen Gunhild had died, and as she alone had restrained King Svein from his wild and warlike impulses, the King was gathering great forces for his descent on England.

Astrid took up her abode in the castle as formerly, but the life was a lonely one. Her parents had died when she was a child, and only her Uncle Halfdan was near her. She disliked King Svein, who, although he always treated her well and kindly, was a moody and irritable man, with no thought for anything save his selfish ambitions. Soon after Astrid's return he placed in her care his two sons, Harald and Canute, and she took great interest in the education and care of the two lonely boys, little thinking that in after days the younger was to prove a great and worthy king of England, thanks to her early teachings.

So the summer passed, while men assembled and were sent on to the Danish settlements in the north of England to wait the arrival of Svein in the fall. Jarl Halfdan was sent in command of one of these detachments, and after his departure Astrid felt her loneliness more than ever.

One day King Svein sent for her. Wondering at the summons, Astrid proceeded to the hall, where she found the king surrounded by his chiefs.

"Lady Astrid," he said abruptly, "prepare your belongings for a journey. Your hand has been asked in marriage by the son of King Vladimir of Russia, and needless to say, I have accepted the offer, for besides being a great honor, this will bring to my army a number of ships from Russia."

Astrid was overwhelmed, but answered the King bravely. "You have no right to dispose of my hand, King Svein, in this fashion! It is unjust to me, for I am not your vassal. My lands lie in Vendland, and if necessary I shall appeal to King Burislaf for protection against this outrage!"

The King's face darkened. "You will do as I order!" he exclaimed angrily. "King Burislaf also will do whatever I order him, and this is a thing unheard of, that a girl should decide her own marriage!"

A murmur of assent went up from the chiefs, and Astrid gazed hopelessly around the circle of fierce faces, finding no hope in them. How she longed for her good uncle to stand at her side! But as the King said, a girl in those days could rarely indeed marry whom she liked; her parents or guardian settled that without consulting her, and Astrid felt that she was helpless.

"This is a noble marriage," continued the King, more calmly, "so let me hear no more of these protests. You will leave here in two weeks for Gardarike, Vladimir's capital, with a fitting escort."

With that the girl was dismissed to her apartments. Young Canute, hearing of the matter, tried to comfort her, but the boy was of course as helpless as she. So, although Astrid resolved that the marriage should never take place, even though she had to fly from home, the packing of her effects proceeded.

A week later, as she was sitting sewing in the garden, she heard a great noise from the harbor, shouts and war-horns mingling with the clash of arms. She sent Canute to see what it was about, and presently the boy came running back, his eyes bright and his cheeks flushed with excitement.

"Oh, Astrid!" he cried, "we have visitors! Two great ships just sailed into the harbor, from far over the sea—the strangest ships! They didn't have any dragon in the bow, but instead was a big gilded cross! All the men on board had shields with red crosses on them, and I saw them as they landed—great warriors, all of them!"

Astrid's cheek paled suddenly. What ships could these be, sailing under the Cross, unless—? Canute continued hastily:

"And, Astrid, you ought to see the chiefs! There is one old viking, so fierce and brave-looking, and a beautiful girl with bright yellow hair, and a boy who must be her brother; but greatest of all was a young man with hair like sunlight, streaming over his shoulders, and a great golden helmet—"

Astrid did not wait to hear the rest. Dropping her work, she ran to her rooms, her heart beating wildly. Swiftly calling her women, she attired herself, and descended to the hall, which was empty. She hastened out, and leaving the castle, went down to the harbor.

There all the townfolk and the men from the castle were crowded about the market place, and as they made way for her respectfully, Astrid saw King Svein talking to a number of people, whom she could not see for the crowd. As she made her way through the press, a well-known voice fell on her ear; and then, with flushed cheek, she found herself face to face with Sigurd Fairhair!

He gave a cry of delight as he saw her, and gripped her hands until they hurt.

"Astrid!"

"Why, Sigurd!" she replied, noting how he had grown, "what a big man you have become already! Oh, how glad I am to see you—and how I need you, too!" she added in a lower tone.

Sigurd gave her a quick, anxious look, then turned. "Here, Alfred, Sigrid!" he shouted, and the next minute the two girls were in each other's arms, while the crowd looked on, amazed.

Sigurd told King Svein something of their tale, then the king ordered all to follow him to the castle.

"We can talk in peace there," he said. "Do you come up at once. My men will attend to your ships, so bring your warriors ashore and let them be entertained at the barracks."

Sigurd left this to Biorn, and the four young people followed Svein to the castle, where they seated themselves in the hall, below the high-seat.

"Now, how do you come to be here, of all places?" asked King Svein, who remembered Sigurd well. In return Sigurd told him about the rescue of Alfred and Sigrid. Svein nodded.

"I know the story. Jarl Alfwic is even now with my army in England. Go on."

"King Olaf," continued Sigurd, "sent Alfred and his sister to you asking that you take them with you to their father; or, if you could not do this, to see that they received a pilot to take them safely to Flanders. However, since you are going to England before long yourself, that is settled."

"Right glad will I be," replied the King, "to have the son of Jarl Alfwic with me. They will be safely delivered to the Jarl, have no fear."

"As to myself," said Sigurd, "that is another matter. King Olaf has sailed for Norway to take the kingdom from Jarl Hakon, and—"

He was interrupted by a cry of amazement from the Danes.

"What say you?" shouted Svein, leaping up, "King Olaf has sailed for Norway? Skoal! Skoal!" The chiefs roundabout echoed the cheer.

"He sent me to you, King Svein, to ask that if possible you will send him ships and men; or, if you cannot do this, that at least you will not aid Jarl Hakon and Jarl Eirik."

"As to the first request, I cannot do that," replied Svein, "for I need every man I can raise. Be sure, however, that Olaf need fear no attack from me; I will be joyful, indeed, when the traitor Hakon is driven from Norway!"

She found herself face to face with Sigurd Fairhair.

"That will be good news for Olaf," rejoined Sigurd, "for an attack in the rear would be fatal. He has but five ships, of which mine is one, and his success will depend entirely on his being able to surprise Hakon."

Sigurd then told of how Olaf had Christianized the Orkneys, and how he had dispatched him immediately on this journey. Olaf was to remain three weeks in the islands, baptizing the people, and had arranged to meet Sigurd at Moster, an island on the west coast of Norway, for which Olaf would direct his course.

Sigurd had no opportunity to speak with Astrid till the evening, and he was puzzled by her words of that morning. Not till Alfred, Sigrid and he went to her apartments in the evening did he receive an explanation. Then Astrid told them about Svein's plans for her marriage.

"It is a shame!" exclaimed Sigrid. "Why, in England a girl must yield obedience to her father's wishes, but she is not forced into marrying in this way!"

Sigurd was silent, his brows knitted. "I am in a bad position," he said at last. "Of course, the simplest way out of it would be for you to come on board the 'Crane,' and for us to join King Olaf; but I am on a mission here that I must not neglect. I cannot anger Svein against Olaf, as such an action would do; not that I care for my own sake, but it might mean ruin to my King."

Alfred agreed with him. "Yes, you must consider your duty to Olaf; and yet there are two sides to it—"

"No," broke in Sigurd, "there are not. At any cost must Svein's finger be kept out of Olaf's pie, for Svein is liable to abandon his English trip and turn all his forces against Norway in a sudden fit of rage. That would be fatal to Olaf at present."

"I think I have a plan," remarked Sigrid after a moment. "As long as you do not appear in Astrid's escape, it will be all right, won't it?"

Sigurd nodded.

"Well then, give Wulf a few men and that cutter that is on the 'Snake,' let them take Astrid on board, and wait for you at some place along the coast. You must leave to-morrow or next day to rejoin Olaf, so you can pick them up as you go, and King Svein will think Astrid has fled of her own will."

"Good!" cried Sigurd. "What say you to the plan, Astrid?"

"I think it is a good one, too," replied the girl, her dark eyes sparkling, "but all my things are packed up, and I don't want to meet King Olaf looking like this!"

She blushed as a peal of laughter went up from the rest.

"Never mind, Astrid," laughed Sigrid, "I will put a chest aboard the 'Crane' tonight; my things will fit you pretty well, and King Olaf gave me a whole shipload of dresses."

"Better put it in the cutter," said Alfred, "for when Svein finds his ward gone, he will search our ships first thing."

So it was arranged, that the next night Wulf, who had firmly attached himself to the young Jarl, should wait at the dock for Astrid, who insisted on making her way down to the harbor alone.

CHAPTER XX

THE KING AND THE TOWEL

NEXT MORNING Wulf was instructed in his part. He had become firmly attached to the young Jarl, and was eager for the business; he and Biorn had proved wise advisors on many occasions.

In the afternoon Sigurd and Alfred went hunting with King Svein, and the party did not return till long after nightfall. When they reached the castle they found the courtyard ablaze with torches.

"What is this? What means this commotion?" roared the King, dismounting hastily and striding forward.

Ulf, the gray-headed old seneschal, met him. "The Lady Astrid of Vendland has disappeared, my lord, and we can find no trace of her in all the castle and town!" For a moment the King's rage was terrible, and he turned on Sigurd, his face working in fury.

"This is your doing, Jarl! You have accepted my hospitality, traitor, and—"

"You forget yourself, my lord," interrupted Sigurd calmly. "I have been with you all day, and could have known nothing of this matter. I do not blame the girl greatly, yet you can account for my actions."

"True," replied Svein, his anger cooling under Sigurd's reply, "I beg your pardon, Jarl, for my haste. Will you allow my men to search your ships? It may be that the girl has fled on board one of them, seeking shelter with the Lady Sigrid."

"Willingly, King," answered Sigurd, Alfred joining with him.

The King at once sent men in all directions, mounted and on foot; but when Sigurd retired for the night nothing had been found of Astrid.

In the morning Sigurd took leave of King Svein, who, preoccupied with the flight of Astrid, offered no hindrance to his departure, presenting him with many gifts, indeed, which Sigurd returned in kind.

His departure was the occasion for a much more sincere and affectionate farewell between himself and the young Saxons. Alfred and Sigrid stood on the deck of the "Crane" till the last moment, and their eyes were moist as they said good-by.

"Be sure to visit us in England next year," were Alfred's parting words. "We will look for you in the summer at Lincoln!"

Sigurd promised to come if possible, and so the three friends parted. As the "Crane" sailed from the harbor Sigurd's last view was of Sigrid, standing on the forecastle of the "Snake" and waving her scarf in farewell.

"Where are we to pick up Wulf and Astrid?" Sigurd asked Biorn, after they had left the land behind.

"About twenty miles north, Jarl. I sent a man with him who knew of a small river mouth where they can lie hid without danger."

Shortly after noon Biorn, taking the helm, steered the "Crane" carefully in to the land, skirting along the shore, and in half an hour the cutter darted out as they passed.

"Hurrah!" shouted Sigurd, as Astrid climbed up the side. "You have done well, indeed, Wulf! King Svein was completely at sea as to where his ward had gone!"

"And now for King Olaf!" cried Astrid merrily, as Wulf carried Sigrid's chest into the cabin and she disappeared.

It was many days before they saw the King, however, for Moster was far up the Norwegian coast. They made the high cliffs of Agdir first, and sailed north along the coast; on the way they passed by Hiorunga Bay, but did not enter, for the place recalled sad thoughts to Sigurd's mind.

"Have you seen Vagn?" he asked Astrid, as they watched the Herey Islands speed by.

"Oh, yes!" she exclaimed. "How could we have forgotten to speak of him before! He came to see me last spring—and just think, Sigurd! He is married!"

Sigurd gave an exclamation of surprise, and Astrid continued.

"Yes, he married a girl in Norway, and brought her back to Denmark. He would have nothing to do with Jarl Sigvald on his return, calling him a coward and a traitor, and the Jarl is remaining close in Jomsborg. Vagn himself is in the south of Denmark, where his father owned some castles."

Sigurd was surprised to hear that his cousin was married, and he firmly resolved to visit him as soon as the result of Olaf's expedition was decided. The next morning they arrived at Moster, and before the fishing village found the four ships of Olaf, which had arrived a few days previously.

Olaf welcomed Astrid back with much merriment. "You seem to come back to your friend Oli," he laughed, "and this time Oli is not going to let you go away so soon!"

Sigurd told him the story of Astrid's flight, and the King commended his Jarl for acting so wisely. "If Svein had come on us now, Fairhair, it would have been all over with us; as it is, you did right in getting the maid away without trouble, and I am heartily glad that you did so."

Olaf stopped at Moster for two days, and as he had first landed in Norway there, he marked out a space on the ground, gave Thangbrand plenty of money and materials, and left him there to build the first church in the country.

After this Olaf sailed north day and night as the wind favored him, following the land, but keeping to the open sea, outside the islands which were strewn thickly along the coast. When the wind was contrary he anchored at the islands farthest out to sea, and did not touch the mainland, for fear that Jarl Hakon would receive news of his coming. At last, just at evening, they reached Agdaness, at the entrance to the Firth of Thrandheim.

After the ships were anchored and the awnings raised, King Olaf visited the "Crane."

"Now, Sigurd," said he, "I wish your advice. Thorir Klakke is on board my ship, and you know how his plans were revealed to me by my brothers, whom he attempted to bribe. Well, Jarl Hakon's men are hidden in the forest yonder, and are doubtless awaiting us; Thorir is to take me ashore alone, as if to arrange some plan of action, and there I am to be killed. Now, what would you suggest doing?"

Thinking it over, Sigurd replied, "It seems to me, Olaf, as that it would be fitting to let the traitor fall into his own trap. Put a score of men ashore to-night, let them hide near by, and when Hakon's men appear let our men charge them and put them to flight, after which Thorir should be executed."

"That is a right good scheme." answered the King. "I do not want to take life, God knows, yet such criminals must be punished; and the most fitting punishment for this man is death. So be it."

Early the next morning Sigurd, watching from the "Crane," saw Thorir and the King go ashore alone. They walked along the shore, then Thorir held up his glove, as if signaling. The next minute a number of men broke from the trees, but as they did so, more men rose up from among the bowlders on the shore and put them to flight. Two of these latter fell on Thorir, while the King watched, and the unfortunate man expiated his treachery with his life.

After this, Olaf, walking down to the water, shouted to Sigurd to come ashore, which the young Jarl did.

"Come, Fairhair, let us walk up and see if we can find a farm, where we can learn tidings of Jarl Hakon. If he is in Thrandheim we must fall upon him to-day or to-morrow at latest, for these men will bear the news of our coming."

They walked up the hill, leaving their men behind, and presently came to a little farmhouse, with a pasture behind it where some cows were grazing. Walking up to the door, they saw an old woman inside, and Olaf addressed her.

"Good dame, may we have a drink of fresh milk? We are two travelers, and will pay for what we take."

"Welcome, friends!" replied the woman. "Enter and I will get some milk and bread."

While she was away, Olaf and Sigurd washed their hands at the well beside the house, and entering again, the King took up a towel that was lying on the table, and dried his hands on it. At that moment the woman returned, and snatched the towel from his hand.

"It is easy to see that you have not been brought up very well, and have been taught little good," she cried angrily. "Know you not that it is wasteful to wet all the towel at once?"

Olaf responded, soberly, "Well, well, mayhap I shall still rise in the world so high that I may dry my hands in the middle of the towel!" Sigurd was bursting with laughter, and at this reply he could hold in no longer, and the woman looked furiously at him.

They drank their milk, and the coin that Olaf handed the woman somewhat appeased her. "Tell me," he asked, "do you know where Jarl Hakon is?"

"Last night he was in hiding, my son told me."

"In hiding! What mean you?" exclaimed the King.

"Why, whence come you that you know not? Within the last few months Hakon has become so cruel and tyrannical that there is no living with him; two days ago his exactions in Gauladale caused the bonders to rise against him, under Orm Lugg. They separated the Jarl from his ships and drove him into the forest, no one knows where. My son told me last night, ere he crossed the Firth to join the bonders, that they were going to look for him at the home of Thora of Rimul, a great lady who is a relative of the Jarls'."

"Well, well!" said the King, as they hastily returned to the ships. "Think you not that heaven is with me, Fairhair? Here I come to Norway at the very moment when Hakon has goaded the bonders to rise in revolt; I find him cut off from his men and ships, driven a fugitive into the forests, mayhap slain by this time! Come, let us make all haste to cross the Firth and arrive at Gauladale."

So, hastily shouting out the news to the other ships as they went on board, the prows were turned across the Firth of Thrandheim, toward the district of Gauladale.

CHAPTER XXI

THE DEATH OF HAKON

AS THEY left the shelter of the bay and drew across the Firth, the narrow entrance of which was only two or three miles in width, three ships were seen sailing along the opposite shore. Olaf steered directly for them, for without doubt these were ships of Hakon's; but as the fleets neared each other, the three ships, evidently taking Olaf's ships for foes, turned toward the shore.

The King dashed forward, coming up with the three ships just as they ran up on a sandbar. Their crews leaped overboard, wading and swimming to shore, and directly in front of Olaf's ship was seen a large, handsome man, swimming. Olaf shouted, but he paid no heed; so, seizing the tiller, the King flung it at him. The heavy missile struck him on the head, and he sank.

Then Olaf's men, leaping overboard, pursued the flying men, slaying some and capturing others. As soon as the captives were brought on board the King interrogated them.

It seemed that the man whom Olaf had slain with the tiller was Erland, a son of Jarl Hakon, and that these ships were going to the Jarl's aid. Further, the prisoners said that Jarl Hakon's forces were utterly dispersed, that the bonders were in revolt throughout the whole district, and that none knew where the Jarl was in hiding.

King Olaf at once landed some of his men with orders to tell everyone who he was, why he had come, and to bid all the bonders meet him the next day in Gauladale. Then the five ships were steered east, going up the Firth, and that afternoon the King was landed at Gauladale.

He found a great meeting of the chief bonders and leaders of the revolt against Hakon in progress, and as soon as these found who he was, they greeted him with tears of joy, and welcomed him most heartily. Olaf brought his chiefs, Sigurd among them, to the assembly, and when all were seated one of the older leaders of the peasants rose and addressed him.

"Olaf, Jarl Eirik will demand stern payment of this attack on his father, Hakon, when he hears of it; nevertheless, we are determined that Jarl Hakon shall die, for his life has been altogether evil. You, however, are of the race of our old Kings, from Harald Fairhair to your father, Triggve, and in the name of this assembly I ask you to become King over us, at least until an assembly of the people can be held at Thrandheim to elect you in regular form."

This caused the men of Olaf much joy, and the King accepted the offer of leadership which they made him. The same evening they traveled up the valley to Rimul, where the Lady Thora lived. It was here that the bonders thought Jarl Hakon was in hiding, but some distance up the valley, beside the river was found a cloak, which was recognized as Jarl Hakon's.

"He has perished in the river!" cried many voices, and this opinion was strengthened by finding the body of Hakon's horse farther down, on a sandbank. But as everyone was discussing this, an old bonder came up to Olaf.

"Olaf," he remarked, "you know well how cunning the Jarl is, and how skilled he is in tricks. A man of his nature does not get carried away by a river, however swift; can you not see that this is but a trick to make us cease the search and disband?"

"That is so," replied Sigurd at once. "I believe the man is right, King."

Others assented to this opinion also, and the small army pushed on to Rimul. By torchlight they made a thorough search of the homestead of Lady Thora, but without avail; so King Olaf, standing on a large stone near the barn, cried out:

"Men, we have searched without avail for Jarl Hakon; at this time we can do no more. But know, that with fitting gift and payment I will reward whoever shall slay the Jarl and bring me his head."

With that they left the homestead, and proceeded to Ladi, where they remained for the night. This was a very large farm and village, belonging to the Kings of Norway, and here Olaf took up temporary quarters. The men were next morning landed from the ships, the bonders were levied, and word was sent throughout the whole country that King Olaf, son of King Triggve, had arrived to take the rule from the hands of Hakon, and that a General Assembly of the People was to meet at once at Thrandheim.

These things, however, were not all done in a day. The very next afternoon, after reaching Ladi, word was brought to King Olaf that a man was inquiring for him, having a large package. King Olaf and Sigurd went to the door of the farmhouse, and saw an ill-favored man wearing the collar of a thrall, or slave.

"What do you want of me?" inquired the King.

For answer the man opened his package and showed a human head. Sigurd could not repress a shudder, and he turned away; the head was that of Jarl Hakon of Norway.

Olaf called his men at once, and the thrall told his story. He was the tooth-thrall of Hakon, the slave, who, according to custom, had been given the Jarl when he cut his first teeth; he had fled with Hakon from the bonders, and the Lady Thora had made for them a sure hiding-place in a cave beneath the pigsty, in the very yard where Olaf had offered a reward for Hakon's head.

"What led you to betray the Jarl?" asked Olaf, angrily.

"Chiefly for the reward you promised, King, for we could hear your voice distinctly. So I slew him as he slept and brought his head to you for the promised reward."

"Seize him, men!" cried Olaf, his eyes blazing with anger as he pointed to the thrall. "I will keep the promise which I made, to give you a fit reward, and it will keep those who come after us from betraying their lords! You dog! You were the servant of a wicked man, but he was your master and a good one to you, and you were bound to him by oaths the most sacred. Your reward shall be a fitting one indeed; take him out and behead him, men!"

When this was done, King Olaf took the thrall's head, together with that of Hakon, and sailing out to the island of Nidarholm, which was used as a place of execution for evildoers, the two heads were placed on the gallows. That night King Olaf gathered his leaders in the farmhouse at Ladi.

"My friends," he said, "Jarl Hakon is dead, and I doubt if Jarl Eirik will dare to attack us. The General Assembly will be held soon, and I trust that the people will take me for their king. It seems to me that only by the aid of God was the mighty Hakon overthrown so easily; moreover, the time is come when idolatry and heathen worship in Norway must give way to the Holy Truth. You have come hither from Ireland with me, and are you now willing to give your lives, if need be, to spread the Word of God?"

"Aye!" shouted all, and after a council it was decided that as soon as Olaf had been chosen king the first steps should be taken to stamp out the worship of Thor and Odin at the great temple in Thrandheim. Sigurd remembered his adventure with Vagn in that temple, and he felt a thrill at thought of planting the Cross in place of the great golden statue of Thor; for the words of the King had fired all his chiefs, and Bishop Sigurd also had spoken at length.

They abode quietly at Ladi for two or three weeks, Astrid taking up her quarters in the big farmhouse. There was nothing to do save to wait till the bonders met in General Assembly, and for this reason also King Olaf waited before tearing down the great temple to Odin at Ladi. It would not be wise to anger the bonders before being elected; afterwards, when he was the rightful King, it would be different.

Finally word arrived that the delegates to the Assembly had met from all eight districts of Norway, so Olaf and his men traveled up to Thrandheim, at the head of the Firth. Olaf was pretty sure of election, for while he dwelt at Ladi most of the great men of the country had visited him, and his handsome presence and kingly mien had made a very favorable impression; moreover, he was well known by reputation as one of the greatest warriors of his time.

Arrived at Thrandheim, Olaf, Sigurd, Astrid and the others of the King's party were given apartments in the palace of Jarl Hakon, and two mornings later they took their way to the Assembly. Here an immense crowd was assembled, from the whole Thrandheim district, and as soon as the Assembly had been constituted, King Olaf stood up in sight of all, his red-gold hair flying in the breeze, the sun streaming from his golden armor and scarlet cloak.

"It is known to all men here assembled that I have offered myself to be King over you. You must expect the sternest treatment by Jarl Eirik for the attack on his father, unless you obtain protection; on the other hand, I have a difficult task before me in obtaining possession of my father's realm, after being so long absent."

Olaf gave a brief account of his life and adventures, from his boyhood up to his discovery of Thorir Klakke's treachery, his coming to Norway, and the death of Hakon, and concluded with:

"I believe that there is no man in Norway who by legal right and descent has so much right to the crown as I. But I must be made King by you, the Assembly of the People, and if you do so I will protect you and rule you according to the ancient laws of Norway."

The tale of his exile and sufferings greatly moved the people, who were already predisposed in his favor. As he sat down, half the delegates leaped to their feet.

"Skoal! Olaf Triggveson, skoal! We will have you to be our King, and none other! Skoal!"

A blare of horns mingled with shouts rent the air, and Sigurd, behind Olaf, set his great standard flapping in the breeze. A silence fell over the people as they saw the Cross, but only for a moment; again the shout arose, pealing across the town and the bay and echoing back from hill to hill behind them:

"Skoal to King Olaf! Skoal!"

CHAPTER XXII

THE SACRIFICE TO THOR

THUS WAS Olaf Triggveson chosen by the General Assembly to be King over all Norway, and the rule of the land was made over to him in accordance with the old laws, by the officers of the people. The bonders swore to be faithful to him, to support him while he won the whole kingdom, and to help him to hold it; Olaf on his part promised to observe the laws and rights of the people, and to defend it from all invaders.

These ceremonies occupied the better part of the day, and it was sunset before Sigurd and Astrid, who had watched the ceremony, returned to the hall. They saw nothing of Olaf for several days, for he was very busy with the various leaders who flocked to his banner, and he was raising men and sending messages to all quarters of Norway with news of his election.

Soon, however, news arrived that the levies were not needed, for Jarl Eirik and his brother Svein had fled to Sweden as soon as the news of their father's death arrived. The whole country yielded to Olaf's rule, glad once more to have a king of the royal line of rulers, and glad to get rid of Hakon, who to this day is known as "Hakon the Bad."

King Olaf was eager to preach the gospel to his people, but Sigurd, his namesake the Bishop, and the other chiefs saw that Olaf must first make his hold on the country firmer, for they foresaw that when the people found that Olaf was intending to overturn the old faith, there would be tumults and revolts. The King, however, yielded only in part to them; and refusing to dwell in Thrandheim, where the great temple of Thor was situated, began the building of a second town, Nidaros, a few miles distant. So the autumn and early winter passed.

Nevertheless, the news spread that Olaf was no follower of the old gods, and grave disturbances took place throughout the country, for the bonders drew away from the new King when they found that he was preaching a new faith to them. Then one day came the news that at many of the larger temples great meetings of the bonders had taken place, with sacrifices to the old gods, and there the bonders had solemnly vowed that they would not allow Olaf to preach the "White Christ" in Norway.

Now all agreed that it was indeed time to act, unless the kingdom was to be endangered. The heart of the country was the district around Thrandheim, where the land was most

This cross he planted over the ruins of the idols.

thickly populated, and where the capital lay; so Olaf realized that if he once established Christianity here, it would not be long before the rest of Norway gave in.

With this object he called another General Assembly at Frosta, near the capital; but as the message went forth, the bonders seized the messengers, and substituted a war-arrow, so that all the chiefs and great leaders assembled with a huge host, armed and ready for war.

Olaf, who came to the Assembly with only Sigurd and a score of men, saw that he was taken in a trap; however, on the first day of the meeting he conciliated the Assembly, although when he mentioned Christ several of the leaders arose and forbade him to speak on religious subjects on that day.

Sigurd saw that the bonders were in a bad mood, and that a spark might inflame them; so that night, as he and King Olaf sat in their tent, he said:

"Olaf, I have a plan which I think will save us all from further trouble."

"Then, by St. Michael, let me have it!" cried Olaf, "for I am at my wits' end for want of one!"

So Sigurd talked long with the King that evening. The next morning, when the Assembly opened, Olaf arose, and after a short speech said:

"Let us preserve the compact that we made before, to strengthen and uphold each other. To this end I will attend your great sacrifice two weeks hence at the temple in Thrandheim, and after this we will take counsel together concerning the faith that will be held, and we will agree to hold to whatever faith we decide upon."

At this the bonders gave a great shout of joy, thinking that King Olaf was yielding, and the other matters for which the Assembly had been called passed off without trouble.

When Olaf returned to his new town of Nidaros a number of men from Iceland received baptism, shortly after Yuletide. Many traders and others who were in the new city of Nidaros, remained through the winter at Olaf's court, and most of these were also baptized in the end.

For the next two weeks both Sigurd and the King were busy perfecting Sigurd's plan. The chief opponent of Christianity among the bonders was Ironbeard, a very powerful chief who was also priest at Moeri, a town near Thrandheim. The winter sacrifice was to be held at the great temple in Moeri, and if Sigurd's plan went well, all resistance to Christianity in the district would be destroyed at one blow.

Invitations were sent out to all the chief men of the bonders, to a feast to be held at Nidaros three days before the winter sacrifice. The greatest chiefs and leaders of the Thrandheim districts were invited, and all accepted, save Ironbeard and one or two others.

On the morning bidden, the invited chiefs streamed into town, on foot, on horseback, and even on skis. Many came over the ice from across the bay, and by next morning the new city was filled with men, as each chief brought a party with him. Early in the morning Olaf and his court attended service in the new church, all the visitors refusing to watch the service.

Immediately afterward Sigurd led fifty men to the harbor. There they put on skates, and the young Jarl led them to Ladi, which was only three miles across the ice, though more by land.

Removing their skates, Sigurd and his men tramped up from the shore to the temple which stood on the hill, and raising his axe, Sigurd struck the door. In five minutes it was broken down, while the few priests who lived near by stood watching helplessly.

Carrying out all the images, Sigurd piled them in the show and set fire to them as an object lesson to the watching priests and bonders that their gods were powerless. The temple was then stripped of its valuables and the building itself burned. When this was done, Sigurd and his men made a cross out of two beams of wood, and this he planted in the snow over the ruins of the idols.

Then, seeing the bonders gathering fast, he stepped out and addressed them:

"Friends, we are here by command of the King, and you have to-day seen how powerless your gods are before the true God. As you know, your chiefs are now in Nidaros; when they return they will be Christian men, no longer heathen."

With this Sigurd and his men, laden with the spoil of the temple, returned to Nidaros. At the harbor mouth a man met them, for it was noontime.

"Hasten, Jarl! The Assembly has just been called!" he cried to Sigurd. "King Olaf posted me here to bid you hasten to the hall."

Sigurd hurried on to the palace, bidding his men wait in the outer rooms till he blew his horn. Then he made his way to the hall, entering it just as the Assembly was opened by the King.

"Chiefs and bonders," said Olaf, looking sternly around on the two score great leaders who sat below his high-seat. "I do not forget that you chose me to be your King, and gave me this realm of Norway; but some two weeks ago I called a General Assembly of the people, and there you and others refused to hear me preach the gospel of Christ, and only by promising to attend the winter sacrifice did I escape injury at your hands.

"Now you and all men know that I have in many places shamed the false gods, burnt their images and temples, and in their stead have erected the Cross of the true God. But I am conscious of the oath which I swore to you at that Assembly, and therefore I propose to sacrifice to your gods the greatest and highest sacrifice that man may offer, namely, human life."

A little murmur of joy ran around the hall as Olaf paused. On great occasions the Norsemen used to offer as the most acceptable sacrifice a number of slaves or criminals, condemned to death. At the next words of Olaf, the joyous murmur ceased.

"I do not believe that thralls or malefactors should be offered to the gods; instead, they should delight in the blood of noble men, great chiefs, powerful bonders. Since you have refused to release me from my oath, I propose to sacrifice this sort of men, for we must do our best to appease the gods, that they may favor us. Am I right?"

As the King paused again, a doubtful murmur of assent rose up, and the men, not quite sure of Olaf's meaning, fixed their eyes on the King, who stood, handsome and erect, by his throne.

"Therefore," he continued, "I will offer to your gods the greatest sacrifice that Norway has ever known. You must be eager to receive from them the reward of your service and past offerings, and for the purpose of this offering I shall select you, Orm Lugg, you, Asbiorn of Orness, you, Stirkar of Gimsa, you, Kar of Gryting, and I will sacrifice you upon the high altar of Thor at Thrandheim. And after this, I shall select six others, the highest and worthiest men of this district from among you, and they shall be sacrificed likewise, that the gods may send us fruitful seasons and peace."

CHAPTER XXIII

HOW THE CHIEFS WERE BAPTIZED

FOR A moment the chiefs stared at the King, incredulous and amazed. Then, as they caught the meaning of his ironic speech, the four men he had named leaped to their feet, and an angry roar went up from all. Olaf's uplifted hand stilled the murmur.

"Wait! You do not seem so eager for the companionship of your gods; can it be that you doubt their power to save you? If that is really the case, and you wish to release me from that oath of mine, I will be right glad to have you all baptized, and believe in the mighty, gentle and kind God whom I and my men serve."

At these words Sigurd blew his horn, and the doors in the side of the hall flew open. His men brought in the spoils of the Ladi temple and laid them at Olaf's feet, while other armed men filed silently into the room.

"Here," exclaimed Olaf, pointing to the temple utensils and trappings, "you see how powerless your gods are to save their belongings! Now think it over, while my men watch the doors; I will return in a few minutes."

With these words he left the hall, followed by Sigurd. Outside the door he gripped the boy's arm joyfully, and was about to speak when an indignant voice broke on their ears;

"What is this tale I hear, King Olaf?" Looking up they saw before them the old English Bishop, Sigurd, clad in his vestments. His face was stern and cold as Olaf bowed to him.

"Is this tale true? That you hold the Thrandheim chiefs in the great hall, offering them their choice of baptism or death? Answer me!"

Astounded, the King gazed at the Bishop, then after a moment his eyes fell.

"Why, Bishop, it is true, certainly! What mean you?"

The old man's eyes flashed. "Think you that this is the way to spread the gospel of Christ? Is baptism a thing to be forced on men, or a thing which they must choose willingly? Better lose this kingdom of yours and flee back over the ocean again than to do this thing, Olaf Triggveson!"

At this the boy spoke out. "Bishop, it is my fault, for I suggested the plan; but why is it so bad? Did not the chiefs entrap Olaf a week or two ago?"

Bishop Sigurd turned on him. "What of that? Do as you will with the bodies of these men, Olaf, but force not their souls! Let them come to Christ willingly." His voice softened. "I know that you both are only overzealous; but believe me, King and Jarl, this is not Christianity. Christ said, 'Come unto me'; think you he would have men driven to him with whips and swords, who died to save men?"

Olaf bent his head, and Sigurd dropped on his knees. "Pardon, Bishop! I had not thought of it that way; I see how wrong it was now!"

The Bishop put his hand on Sigurd's head. "And you, Olaf? Do you not see that I am right? Must you be led by this boy?"

Olaf, fixing his keen eyes on the old man, nodded slowly. "I see, Bishop, and I will obey your unspoken thought."

He turned slowly, and Sigurd followed him to the door of the great hall. As they entered there was a hush, and Olaf curtly bade his men leave the building, waiting in silence as they filed out.

Then, ascending the high-seat, he said bitterly:

"Chiefs, I came among you preaching the Word of God, the gospel of peace and salvation; but my own acts have been as those of a pagan and worse. Small wonder that you refused to accept my faith! Too late I see that I have done ill by you; now I stand ready to repair my faults, and to act as a true Christian. Go in peace; those of you who wish to accept Christianity will be welcomed. If it is your wish that a heathen King rule over you, I will return whence I came, and will bring no fire and sword into the land."

The chiefs gazed in amazement at the King, and Orm Lugg, one of the greatest spoke out;

"Is this truth, King? Are we free to go to our homes?"

"Yes," said Olaf, a flush mounting to his brow. "I have proved myself a poor Christian, friends, but forgive me for this time; go, and whatever is your will I shall abide by it."

One by one, silent, incredulous, the chiefs left the hall, and Sigurd alone remained with the King. Then the boy, grasping Olaf's hand, cried with tears in his eyes: "Olaf, we have been wrong, but how you must suffer! Will you really go back to Ireland if the chiefs refuse to accept the gospel?"

"Yes, my friend," and Olaf's tone was very low and soft. "The good Bishop yonder showed me more in that minute than I can tell you. I have been proud, Sigurd, and my pride is shattered; the Hammer of Thor is not like Christ's Cross. I thought to use the Cross like a weapon, like Thor uses his Hammer; but the Cross is a symbol, not of pride and might, but of gentleness, of pity, of humility. Yes, my—"

Suddenly the doors opened, and in came the chiefs, to the King's amazement. Their faces were very changed now; the fierceness, the resistance, seemed to have given way to some new emotion.

"King Olaf," said Orm, the spokesman, "we found it as you said; the palace is unguarded, the streets are clear. Oh, King, I have a hard thing to say, but mayhap you will understand! Listen.

"We bonders have in truth resisted your faith because, as you said just now, you preached one thing to us, and you acted another thing. We have resisted, not because we love the old gods; but because we could not see wherein the White Christ was better."

Orm paused, fixing his eyes on the King's. "But to-day, King Olaf, you have shown us a new thing. We have not known you long, yet we have found in you a strong man, a proud man, a man used to ruling the wills of others, and for this we have rejoiced in a worthy King. To-day, Olaf, we have found that there was one thing stronger than these, a thing able to overcome all your strength, pride—even your will; and because this is so, we freely accept from your hand the Cross of Christ."

For a moment Olaf gazed at the men around him, unable to speak. Then, the tears flowing down his cheeks, he pressed their hands, one by one, and said:

"My friends, this is a victory where I had found a defeat. I cannot tell you what it means to me, but I think that none of us will forget this day. Jarl Sigurd and I have to-day learned a lesson from you and from ourselves; pray God we may never have to learn it over again!"

Then Sigurd summoned the Bishop, telling him what had happened on the way, and without delay the chiefs were baptized in Olaf's new church, together with their men. That night Olaf and Sigurd sat in Astrid's chamber, talking over the events of the day until late.

King Olaf had given Astrid part of Jarl Hakon's forfeited estates, to compensate her for those she possessed in Vendland, so that she might be able to live as became her dignity; further, he constituted himself her ward, although with the laughing declaration that he would run the risk of forcing her to marry against her will. He had also promised to give Sigurd an earldom, as soon as he had put the country into some kind of order.

"What are now your plans, my lord?" asked the girl, that same night. Olaf shook his head.

"Truly, Astrid, I know not. Practically all of the greater chiefs from the Thrandheim districts were baptized to-day, and I think that the bond established between us will never be broken. Ironbeard alone holds out; I am strongly minded to visit him at once, during the winter sacrifice, and try to win him over. To-morrow, Sigurd, we will go to Thrandheim and demolish the great temple there."

For a minute Sigurd looked at Olaf, then the latter smiled. "No, Sigurd, I have learned my lesson. There will be no bloodshed, either there or at the winter sacrifice, if I can help it. But the greatest chiefs have been baptized; now it is essential that Ironbeard be either forced to accept my rule or leave the country."

So, without the least opposition, Olaf and Sigurd burned the old temple of the war-god the very next day. Many of the chiefs so recently baptized showed their sincerity by joining Olaf or sending men to his aid; and the idols were taken out before all the people, and burned. Sigurd longed for Vagn to be there, as he remembered their adventure with Jarl Hakon; but his cousin was far away to the south.

The work was finished by midday, and the party returned to Nidaros. The sudden conversion of their greatest chiefs seemed to have demoralized the bonders, for no longer were threats heard against Olaf, but instead, many of them came to Nidaros and were baptized by the good Bishop.

The day after the destruction of the Thrandheim temple, Olaf prepared to go to Moeri, where the winter sacrifice was held. He took all his men, sailing up Thrandheim Firth with his largest ships, and came to Moeri the day of the sacrifice.

The King sent Sigurd ashore, demanding that the people first hold an Assembly. Fairhair found a great multitude assembled from all the countryside, with Ironbeard and his men all present. They at once agreed to Olaf's demand, so the King landed with his men, and the Assembly was constituted on the plain before the temple.

When the noise and talking of the opening had subsided, Olaf arose in his seat and told the bonders what had taken place in his hall at Nidaros, told them how he had found his mistake, and would no longer try to force a religion on them that they did not want.

Sigurd could see a change sweep over the faces of the bonders before him, and they glanced at each other and began whispering. At this, however, Ironbeard leaped to his feet—an immense man, wearing the robes of a priest of Thor, and with an iron-gray beard that swept over his chest. He lifted his hand and began to speak, slowly and with great dignity.

CHAPTER XXIV

OLAF'S ATONEMENT

"KING OLAF," rang out the priest's deep voice, "we are unwilling that you should violate our religion. The wish of us all is that you should offer sacrifice as other kings before you have done, and even as Jarl Hakon did. When King Hakon, foster son of King Athelstan of England, wished to proclaim the White Christ, he found the bonders too strong for him, and he yielded to the old faith. The only proper plan for you is to do likewise, for our minds have not changed since that Assembly wherein you promised to visit this temple at this time."

Ironbeard sat down, and his speech was loudly applauded by the bonders who sat around, and by the great crowd without. Olaf flushed at the chiefs proud demands, but controlling his temper, he rose.

"My friends, I promised to visit your temple, and I shall do so now, before the sacrifices. The Assembly is closed."

With this he motioned to Sigurd, and, followed by his men, who had laid aside their arms, he walked to the door of the temple. Olaf held in his hand a gold-mounted staff of heavy wood, and as they entered he said to Sigurd:

"Jarl, do just as I do, and act quickly."

Inside they saw many images around the temple, and occupying the place of honor was a large idol, heavily adorned with gold and silver. The temple was now full of Olaf's men, while Ironbeard and the bonders stood in the doorway, watching him.

Without another word the King walked up to the large idol, and raising his heavy staff, struck it. The idol toppled over, fell to the stone floor, and broke in two parts. At the same instant Sigurd and his men rushed at the other images and swept them from their pedestals.

A loud cry of horror arose from the bonders, and Ironbeard, seizing a spear, poised it, in the act of hurling it at the King. As he did so, one of Olaf's men, who was outside, pierced him with an arrow, and he fell at the temple threshold.

The bonders drew back, in terror, and the King turned angrily.

"Who fired that arrow?" he shouted. The man who had done so stepped to the door.

"It was I, King Olaf, and I did it to save your life. Ironbeard had poised a spear at you—see, it is even now in his hand!"

Olaf looked at the fallen leader, and saw that the man spoke truly. "Order the Assembly called," he said to Sigurd. "Bid them have no fear."

When the people had taken their places again, Olaf came out of the temple and addressed them from the steps:

"Friends and bonders, I did not come here to shed blood, and I am bitterly grieved that Ironbeard drew his fate on himself. As I told you a little time ago, I will compel no man to leave his faith; I have discovered the wickedness of that course. But a few days ago your other chiefs, some of whom stand at my side, accepted from my hands the Cross of Christ, and now I offer it to you also.

"You have seen how your gods have fallen and broken. Where is their power, think you? The true God has protected me, has brought me to this kingdom and given it into my hand without a struggle, and whether you will it or not, his faith will prevail in Norway before many more years have passed."

The King paused, and one of the bonders arose to reply.

"Oh, King, your words to-day have fallen pleasantly on our ears, and we easily perceive that you have truth and justice in your heart. We see, too, that the gods are dead, and that they have no power before the Cross of the White Christ. But, King Olaf, the slaying of Ironbeard was an evil deed, whether you intended it or not, and before we say more on this subject we would like to know whether you will punish his murderer."

The bonder sat down amid a faint murmur of applause, and the Assembly fixed their eyes on Olaf. For a moment the King sat in silence, and it was evident that he was struggling with himself; then his face cleared.

"My people, I will not punish the man, for he saved my life. Wait! I am not through. Are there any relatives of Ironbeard present?"

Two men stood up. "We are distant relatives of his, oh, King, but he has left no others to mourn him save a single daughter."

King Olaf took off his helm. "My people, this is a lawful Assembly, able to give judgment and to punish criminals, with power to inflict penalty for offenses. I appoint you two bonders judges, and I take upon my own head the blood of Ironbeard. Whatever you shall think right, I will agree to, in compensation for his death. Whether you demand my life, or my exile, or a scat in money, these will I give, and you shall fear no punishment from my men."

At these words a silence fell on the host, and Sigurd gazed at Olaf in love and admiration. Truly, old Bishop Sigurd had not spoken in vain! A murmur of appreciation of Olaf's generous offer passed from mouth to mouth, and presently the two relatives of Ironbeard, after conferring together, stood up.

"King Olaf, by these words of yours you have indeed shamed us, who came to this Assembly with arms, and with war in our hearts. It is a new departure in Norway, that her Kings should offer themselves under the laws like common men; and yet it seems not unfair to us that you should do so. The laws declare that for the shedding of blood the relatives of the dead man may claim the life of the slayer, or they may claim a scat in lands or goods. Now, King Olaf, Ironbeard has left no family save a daughter, who has no lack of wealth and is of good family. We, therefore, her relatives, lay this judgment upon you: that you make her your lawful wife and bestow upon her lands befitting her position as Queen."

The King's men uttered a growl of protest, even Sigurd looking somewhat blank, for the King had thought of marrying one of the daughters of the Swedish King, to make an alliance between the two nations. Olaf, however, checked the murmur with a gesture, and replied to the bonders:

"My friends, this is a lawful judgment, and I accept it with good will. I will expect you two men to look to it that the maid is sent to Nidaros before Eastertide, at which time I shall marry her and make her the Queen of this land. It is the least I can do, methinks, after my men have killed her father and left her alone in the world. Should this plan not meet with her consent, I will expect you to appoint other penalty, which I will fulfill most faithfully, and this I swear on the Cross."

Olaf sat down amid a shout of approval and joy from the bonders, and a dozen men rose at once to speak. Making one of their number spokesman, he addressed the King.

"My lord, when I left home it was my firm intention to resist your faith to the last drop of my blood; but now I am proud to take baptism from your hands, and to swear anew my allegiance to you."

Olaf started up in surprise, and one by one the other bonders rose and declared their intention to be baptized. Then Olaf sent for Bishop Sigurd, whom he had left at the ships, fearing that Ironbeard might attack him, and turned to the bonders.

"My people, nothing that you could do would give me more pleasure than this thing. It is the dearest wish of my heart that this land of Norway should become Christian, and once you and the other leaders of Thrandheim and the districts around have received baptism, we will meet with little opposition from the rest of the land. In pledge of your earnestness I ask that you complete the destruction of this your temple to the old gods, and on its site I will erect at my own expense a church to the true God."

Shouting and clashing their arms, the bonders sprang up without an instant's hesitation. They ran to the temple, carried out the broken images, and piled them in the snow, while others stripped the temple of its furnishings and set fire to it. As the pile of idols broke into flame, old Bishop Sigurd arrived from the ships.

He had been told the whole story on the way up the hill, and he gripped Olaf's hand silently but heartily as the King met him. At once the work of baptism was begun, Sigurd and the rest of the King's men taking part in the service, and standing as godfathers to the new converts.

When this was finished the afternoon was nearly spent, and after arranging with the leaders of the people for the building of a church, for the burial of Ironbeard, and for the sending of his daughter Gudrun to Nidaros at Easter, Olaf's men embarked, and the King sailed back down the Firth to Nidaros.

A few days before this the Firth had opened, for although it was still winter, the weather had warmed somewhat, and a channel had been made from above Moeri to the open sea. When the fleet came to the harbor that night, they found the town alight with torches, and lying in the harbor were several newly arrived ships, or rather cutters, for they were small.

"I wonder what this means?" said the King, as they drew into the anchorage. "I had no tidings of visitors, when we left the city yesterday, and it is strange that the town is all alight!"

So before the ships had come to anchor, Olaf and Sigurd leaped into a small boat and were rowed ashore. Their ships had been seen entering, for great fires were lit on either side of the harbor, making everything plain to the sight, and a crowd of men met them as they landed.

"What is all this excitement about?" demanded the King, looking around in wonder.

A confused talking answered him. "Here, one at a time!" shouted Olaf, and one of the men stepped to his side.

"We have been driven from home, my lord King, and we come from the north. There two chiefs, Raud the Strong and Thori Hart, have revolted against the White Christ, have gathered a fleet, and are sailing against you. They are preparing to restore the temples of Thor and Odin and to burn the churches you have built; we, who are Christians, have barely escaped with our lives, fleeing in our small boats. The heathen will enter the Firth in a few days, unless you meet them first!"

CHAPTER XXV

THE WRESTLING MATCH

OLAF AT once went to the great hall, and there the fugitives came before him and told their story. The two Northern chieftains had taken advantage of the unexampled spell of warm weather to raise a fleet and sail down the coast, thinking to come upon the King just as he had come upon Jarl Hakon.

Olaf quickly consulted with Sigurd, the Bishop, and his other leaders, and their opinion was that not a minute was to be lost. If the King embarked that night and sailed out of the Firth, he would reach the entrance by morning, and could wait for the heathen fleet there.

The King agreed to this plan, and at once sent word to his men to return on board the ships. The Thrandheim chiefs now proved their loyalty by refusing to return to their homes.

"No, King," said they, "you have dealt with us fairly and honorably, and we are sensible of it. We and our men will be of use if it comes to a battle, and the enemy may lose heart when they see us, for evidently they count on our forces joining them. So set up our standards on your ships, and we will gladly accompany you."

At this decision the King was overjoyed, for with these men were several hundred warriors in all, who had gathered at the Moeri Assembly. So a few hours later Olaf and Sigurd left Nidaros again, with a dozen ships, while more would follow as soon as they had been taken off their winter dry-docks.

The ships rowed down the Firth all night, while Olaf and Sigurd rested. The day had been a terribly hard one on both, and they were glad to get what sleep they could before meeting the advancing foes.

The week of warm weather seemed a wonderful thing to all the men, and not a few ascribed it to the favor of heaven upon Olaf. It was only barely past Yuletide, and although no one expected the warm weather to last, few of the oldest men could remember a winter when Thrandheim Firth had remained open, or had opened before April.

By morning they were outside the cape of Agdaness, where the traitor Thorkel had been executed. The King ordered the ships to be hove to here, in order to wait for the six other ships which were following from Nidaros. All day long they waited, seeing nothing of the rebels. Two or three small ships, bearing more fugitives, came down the coast, and gave Olaf the news that Raud and Thori were only fifteen miles to the north, that they had landed at Theksdale, and were summoning men to join them from all the country.

That afternoon the reënforcements came up from Nidaros, and the King held a council on his ship the "Crane."

"First," he said, "I am resolved that if it can possibly be avoided there shall be no bloodshed in this matter. Now let me have your council on how we shall act to gain these rebels over, if that can be done."

Sigurd spoke first. "It may be that you did not note it, King Olaf, but old Biorn, my forecastle man, is strongly of the opinion that to-night a heavy frost will set in. This warm weather has not been natural at all; even this afternoon the sun has been growing somewhat colder.

"Now, if a frost returns to-night, it will be no light one, and Biorn says that the Firth will again be closed to us. In this case, it seems to me that any ships lying along the shore would be frozen fast, especially if they were in such a narrow bay as that at Theksdale. I think that Raud and Thori will give little heed to their ships, drawing them on shore carelessly, or perhaps anchoring them near by; and if this is the case, and we come upon them suddenly, they will probably be so disheartened at the loss of their ships, and at being left so far from home without means of retreat, that they will give in."

A cry of delight broke from the King and the others. "That is the very solution of it!" exclaimed Olaf. "But—it depends on whether or not a frost sets in. In any case we will leave the land, so as not to be frozen in ourselves."

The chiefs separated to their respective vessels, and all sailed out two or three miles to sea, where they lay tossing quietly. At sunset Bishop Sigurd, who was aboard the "Crane," conducted a solemn service, during which he offered a solemn prayer that God would favor their enterprise; as the men on all the ships joined in the responses, it seemed to Sigurd Fairhair that never had he witnessed a more impressive sight than this. Eighteen ships, all crowded with men, a large portion of whom had only a few days before been worshipers of idols, lay grouped together in the sunset glow, while from them arose a devout and heartfelt prayer to the White Christ.

No sooner had the sun set and darkness fallen upon the ocean, than the night turned bitterly cold. Many of the men, not expecting this, had left off their furs and cloaks, so that the others divided theirs among all. In some of the ships were bales of merchandise, and at the King's order these were opened by torchlight and all the men without cloaks were furnished with them.

By midnight it was evident that the intense cold would close the Firth, and as Sigurd had foreseen, would also hold the enemy helpless. Amid a shout of rejoicing from all the men, the prows were turned north, and the ships rowed swiftly toward Theksdale, for there was not a breath of wind, and every minute the cold seemed to increase.

With sunrise the pilots announced that they were not far from their goal, and an hour later they rounded the islands outside Theksdale Bay. There, however, they were stopped by a ragged line of ice, nearly a foot thick, which had formed during the night.

In all haste, for as yet they had not come around the headland into the bay itself, the crews disembarked without mishap, and gained the shore, leaving men on board the ships to keep them safe. They made their way, under guidance of men who knew the coast, across the headland; and there before them lay the army of revolt, their fleet fast-bound in fetters of ice along the shore!

"Come," exclaimed Olaf to his nearest leaders, "we must lose no time, for, see, they are cutting the ships out of the ice!"

So, leading the way, he dashed over the rocks of the shore, and as the first shouts of alarm went up from the heathen army, Olaf and part of his men stood between them and their ships, while over the brow of the hill poured the remainder of his forces.

Olaf and his men stood between them and their ships.

The rebel camp seethed and boiled with men, but seeing that Olaf made no move to attack them, their haste quieted somewhat, and in a few minutes two well-appareled chiefs left the tents and with a dozen men approached the King.

"Have we safe conduct, King Olaf?" shouted one.

"Have no fear," replied Olaf, "come in peace."

As they approached, men who knew them whispered to the King that these were Raud the Strong and Thori Hart. Both were of lofty stature and magnificently built, with strong, vigorous features. They stopped a dozen paces from the King.

"From your appearance you are Olaf Triggveson," said one. "I am Raud the Strong, and this is Thori Hart. Have you come in peace or in war, oh, King?"

A smile ran around Olaf's men, and he himself laughed outright.

"That is a strange question, Raud, when you have attacked my people and declared your intention of driving me from the land!"

The other two flushed, and Raud's face darkened. "You have caught me," he cried angrily, "by fault of the ice, King, where my men can ill defend themselves, and I see that you have many more warriors than I looked for; yet you will not find me the last to cross swords with you, Olaf!"

"Hold, Raud," answered Olaf, "I mean not to attack you. Now see, I have your ships yonder, I have a much larger force than you, and yet if you will not yield willingly to me you shall depart in peace to your homes, on condition simply that you abandon the revolt against my rule."

"Why," cried Thori Hart in wonder, "we thought that you made choice of the Cross or the sword to your subjects! Mean you that we will not be forced to baptism?"

Olaf smiled sadly. "You will not, Thori. All the chiefs in the Thrandheim districts have been baptized, but willingly, as those with me here can testify. Now, what is your decision?"

The two whispered together for a minute, until finally Raud spoke up, advancing toward the King.

"You have fairly overcome us, King Olaf, and we thank you for our lives. Still, I am not ready to accept your faith. I am a great priest of Thor in the north, and you seem to be the champion of the White Christ, so I propose that you and I pray to our gods, and after that we indulge in a wrestling match. The winner, he who first throws the other to earth, shall bestow his faith on all the men of the loser. This Thori and I agree to, if you will also."

Olaf, without hesitation, replied, "I will accept the trial, here and now, trusting to the mercy of Almighty God that he will nerve my arm against your power and that of your false gods!

"But one condition I would make, Raud; that is, that whoever loses this contest shall forfeit his life with it."

The viking joyfully agreed, and then returned to his camp. The men of King Olaf had all arrived, and as word of the challenge passed through the army, more than one covert smile was seen, for already men said that Olaf was the strongest man in all the land.

It was so bitterly cold that a great fire was built, and on one side of the space, scraped clear of snow, marked out for the match, grouped Olaf's men; on the other side the heathen followers of Raud stood, full of confidence in their leader, for he was very strong, whence his name, and skilled in wrestling.

Stepping into the open space between the two armies, Olaf and Raud threw off their helmets and armor, and took hold of each other.

CHAPTER XXVI

THE CROSS AND THE HAMMER

SIGURD'S HEART sank as he saw the mighty muscles and powerful limbs of the pagan; but he glanced at Olaf, and while the latter's muscles were not so big, he knew that there was terrible strength in them.

At first the opponents tried out each other carefully; then, gradually warming up, Raud made terrific attempts to throw Olaf, but the latter resisted every endeavor, seemingly without effort. Now was seen the difference in the two men's lives, for while Raud speedily lost his wind, became flushed and tired,

King Olaf looked as fresh as when he began the conflict, owing to his temperate life.

As the viking weakened, Olaf suddenly seized him by the thigh in an unguarded moment, and with a movement of his hands flung the man over his head. Amid a shout from his men, and a groan of dismay from those of Raud, the latter struck the ground, Olaf leaping to his side.

As the fallen man struggled up, the King seized his hand and aided him. "You have won fairly, Olaf," gasped Raud, looking with wondering eyes on his antagonist, "and my life is yours."

"Nay," said the King, kindly, handing the viking his garments, "I seek no man's blood, Raud. All I ask is that you serve me faithfully, and you shall have the same lands that you held from Hakon."

Messengers were at once despatched overland to Nidaros, to tell of the outcome of the conflict; then, after Raud, Thori and his men had been baptized, for they accepted the condition willingly, Olaf embarked his men again and they returned south.

The Firth was of course closed again, so the ships were drawn ashore for the winter, and the chiefs of the bonders left the King for their homes, while he pushed on across the snow-clad hills with his own men. At Ladi they crossed the ice to Nidaros, and were received with much joy.

At Eastertide the marriage of King Olaf and Gudrun, the daughter of Ironbeard, was solemnized by Bishop Sigurd; and at the same time Sigurd Fairhair and Astrid were married. The wedding was a surprise to no one, as the whole court knew the story of their adventures, and had long since agreed that sooner or later the two would be wedded.

Easter of this year came late in April, and the Firth had been open for some time. As the procession left the church and wended through the streets of Nidaros to the great hall, a wonderful ship was seen entering the harbor. The prow ended in a dragon's head, the stern in the coils and tail of a dragon; both prow and stern were gilded, shining bravely in the morning sun. The hoisted sail represented a dragon's wings, and the glistening oar blades the beast's legs.

A cry of amazement went up from all, but the King turned, with a smile at Sigurd.

"This ship I have had built in secret, and it is my wedding gift to my faithful Jarl, Sigurd Fairhair. It is not fitting that a Jarl of mine should be landless, so I also bestow on him the earldom of the Agdirs, and command that he take his wedding journey thither in this his new ship!"

FOUR YEARS later King Olaf Triggveson, with a few of his ships, was entrapped by the treacherous Jarl Sigvald among the islands of Svold Sound, while the main part of his fleet was out at sea.

Here had gathered his enemies—the King of Sweden, King Svein, of Denmark, who had turned against Olaf, and the heathen men of Norway, who had chosen rather to leave the land than to accept the Cross. One by one the King's ships were taken, although he made such a defense as Norway had never seen, and at one time it seemed as though he would win, even against such odds. Then Jarl Eirik, the son of Jarl Hakon, tore the dragon-prows from his ships, and rowed to the attack under the sign of the Cross.

As the last of King Olaf's men fell on his forecastle, the King threw aside his shield and sprang overboard. He was famous as a swimmer through all the lands of the north, and now he dived deeply, swimming under the keels of his enemies' ships, so that it seemed to them that he had drowned.

Coming up outside the ring of vessels, the King swam swiftly to a fishing boat that lay in by the islands, and was pulled aboard by Sigurd and his wife Astrid, who had come too late to warn Olaf of the plot to betray him. That night, with his wounds bound, the King sat in the stern of the boat, which sailed swiftly south.

Sigurd urged Olaf to go north, offering to take him to his fleet, which could return and meet the invaders, but the King refused.

"No, my friends, I cannot do this. Toward the end of the fight Jarl Eirik hoisted the Cross, and I believe he made a vow that he and his men would renounce the old gods forever if he conquered me. Therefore, it seems to me that by the will of God, Norway has become Christian at last, and also I am not without fear that God has been displeased with my rule."

"Then shall we go to England with you? You have many great friends there, and King Ethelred, who is almost driven from his kingdom by the Danes, would gladly give you a share of his realm," said Astrid. Again the King shook his head.

"No," he replied, "let me be as dead to the realm of Norway, for I will never trouble it again. I will go to Rome, and after that to Jerusalem. There the Crusaders rule the Holy Land, and I will join them and devote the rest of my life to serving against the Moslem. I believe that God used me as an instrument for giving his Word to Norway, and now that this is accomplished, it were best to give peace to this troubled realm."

Seeing that it was useless to urge Olaf further, Sigurd sadly gave up, and two days later they arrived in his earldom of Agdir. Here the King remained for two weeks, then, fearing that his presence would bring trouble on his old friends, decided that he would at once start on his pilgrimage.

"Make your peace with the conquerors, Sigurd," he said. "They will be glad to retain you in your possessions here."

With this he selected a score of men and a small ship of Sigurd's, and departed from Norway forever. As he and Sigurd and Astrid stood together on the forecastle, just as the anchor was raised, the King said sadly:

"My friends, it is for the best, believe me, and now peace will come to the land. The faith of Christ has been established, and although men may return at times to the old gods, I think that it will not be for long. Now take this sword of mine, even as you took one long ago in Ireland, and wear it in memory of me; I will never use a weapon again, save in defense of the Holy Land."

Embracing the King with tears, Sigurd and Astrid left the ship; and an hour later it was a white speck far on the horizon.

"Come, Astrid," said Sigurd, "we will never see Olaf again; yet he will always be remembered as the first King of Norway to overthrow the Hammer of Thor, and to plant in its stead the Cross of Christ!"

ABOUT THE AUTHOR

H. BEDFORD-JONES is a Canadian by birth, but not by profession, having removed to the United States at the age of one year. For over twenty years he has been more or less profitably engaged in writing and traveling. As he has seldom resided in one place longer than a year or so and is a person of retiring habits, he is somewhat a man of mystery; more than once he has suffered from unscrupulous gentlemen who impersonated him—one of whom murdered a wife and was subsequently shot by the police, luckily after losing his alias.

The real Bedford-Jones is an elderly man, whose gray hair and precise attire give him rather the appearance of a retired foreign diplomat. His hobby is stamp collecting, and his collection of Japan is said to be one of the finest in existence. At present writing he is en route to Morocco, and when this appears in print he will probably be somewhere on the Mojave Desert in company with Erle Stanley Gardner.

Questioned as to the main facts in his life, he declared there was only one main fact, but it was not for publication; that his life had been uneventful except for numerous financial losses, and that his only adventures lay in evading adventurers. In his younger years he was something of an athlete, but the encroachments of age preclude any active pursuits except that of motoring. He is usually to be found poring over his stamps, working at his typewriter, or laboring in his California rose garden, which is one of the sights of Cathedral Cañon, near Palm Springs.

www.ingramcontent.com/pod-product-compliance
Lightning Source LLC
LaVergne TN
LVHW010620100826
845148LV00014B/3048